THE STORY OF

Creation

The Revelations of Connie Ann Valenti

told to

Monsignor Ronald P. Lengwin

ISBN 978-1-64515-790-8 (paperback)
ISBN 978-1-64515-791-5 (digital)

Christian Faith Publishing, Inc.
832 Park Avenue
Meadville, PA 16335
www.christianfaithpublishing.com

Printed in the United States of America

CONTENTS

ABOUT CONNIE VALENTI

Connie Valenti is a mother and grandmother who sees goodness and beauty in all of life. Sensing God's presence and love in every person and event, she believes the biblical story of Jesus's life and teaching continues to take on deeper meaning and understanding in the circumstances of our daily existence. We are still living the story of Jesus and, now with this book, revelations informing the entire story of creation and what is to come in our world.

Her revelations figured prominently in explaining the forces of evil at work in *The Demon of Brownsville Road: A Pittsburgh Family's Battle with Evil in Their Home* by Bob Cranmer and Erica Manfred.

Connie Valenti has previously written the book, *Stories of Jesus: A Gospel of Faith and Imagination,* together with Monsignor Ron Lengwin, who, for over thirty years, has featured Connie's stories of faith and imagination on his weekly radio show, *Amplify,* on KDKA Pittsburgh. Monsignor Lengwin has been instrumental in cataloguing the revelations contained in this book.

Before the Beginning

by Donald Marinelli, PhD

The Nicene Creed, the most universally accepted and recognized statement of Christian faith, first adopted in AD 325 at the Council of Nicea when the Roman Emperor Constantine sought to unify the Christian church with one doctrine, begins with the words: "I believe in one God, the Father almighty, maker of heaven and earth, of all things visible and invisible..."

And while those words are true, the reality of existence, of universes and humankind, of origins and divine plan, of what has always been, what transpired before there was the dynamic we call time, as well as what will be is much more complicated than posited in the creed.

We begin by affirming the very first statement of the creed: "I believe in one God..." There is in fact one sole God, a divine presence and omniscient power beyond our limited human comprehension. We shall call him The One, the "be all and end all" of everything. His name reflects the vibrations of energy radiating from his being.

While affirming the words of the Nicene Creed as indeed being true, there is much more to be discerned and revealed. Indeed, this is part of the great mystery of The One, of creation, and of being.

As befitting The One, however, the creations of this divine being, who is three in one, are at the same time complex yet simple. They emulate much of what we experience of life on Earth: procreation, diversity, identity, familial devotion, but also jealousy, avarice, and familial conflict. This makes the maxim of humankind being made in God's image tangible in ways never before imagined or comprehended.

Not only was humankind formed in the image of The One, but so was our universe. In fact, the profile of The One is being made more visible by the latest revelations of science and technology. When we see the images captured by the Hubble Telescope, we see a reflection of the divine.

A recent solar eclipse allowed us to see the corona emanating from our sun. Corona means "crown," and what we saw was basically a crown of light and energy emanating from our life-giving star, similar to the love emanating from The One. We see in our universe stars being born out of celestial dust contracting into hot dense cores as they come to life.

Few are those who were not amazed when the Hubble Space Telescope revealed the now iconic image of primal formation called the Pillars of Creation. These elephant trunks of interstellar gas and dust in the Eagle Nebulae allow us to see celestial gestation in action, albeit almost seven thousand light years from Earth and therefore a vision from roughly one thousand years ago!

Out of this same dust is formed the star's family of planets, asteroids, and comets. What is left over remains as space cinders and grit. Seeing this as a preview and reflection of the creative process that led to our planet, our world, and, ultimately, even our Heaven becomes apparent. The more science reveals what was previously unseen, the more a Divine Plan becomes credible.

Wondering how The One, who in truth, is more than a God, could, through force of love, bring forth entities from the same energy, but distinct from us, is manifest in the astronomical dynamic of solar flares. Solar flares occur when magnetic energy has built up in the solar atmosphere and is released suddenly. Solar flares are often accompanied by coronal mass ejections. These magnificent magnetic loops of solar fire and flame are called "prominences" an appropriate term in more ways than one. In a solar flare, radiation is emitted across virtually the entire electromagnetic spectrum. It impacts all aspects of existing matter and energy within range of these flares.

The One's "solar flare and coronal mass ejection," however, is intentional and meaningful. It has the purpose of bringing into existence spiritual entities throughout the universe, or maybe even universes. If ever we needed reinforcement to the theory that seeing is believing, observing the Pillars of Creation was that for many.

In the course of the revelatory journey of this book, we will discover how The One, the embodiment of mystery, has woven for us a life of mystery where clues await discovery by science, sight, and/or divine revelation and love. It calls to mind the musings of Charles Darwin, who wrote: "It occurred to me, in 1837, that something might perhaps be made out of this question [of the origins of species] by patiently accumulating and reflecting on all sorts of facts which could possibly have any bearing on it." Out of this "accumulating and reflecting" came his groundbreaking work on evolution, an accepted scientific fact not at all antithetical to the workings of a mysterious One.

We know from the teachings of Jesus, who truly is the savior of humankind, that God is love and that love is an energy as powerful, real, strong, tangible, and meaningful between The One's sentient creations, as gravity is between all matter, matter generated likewise by The One: the ultimate creator "of all things visible and invisible."

Furthermore, and perhaps shockingly, The One did not reside in "Heaven" when all this happened. There was no Heaven, no distinction between love and place.

This notion and description of The One is very much in keeping with the recent work of American analytic philosopher and Christian apologist, William Lane Craig. Craig first posited the existence of an uncaused, beginningless, changeless, timeless, spaceless, immaterial being of enormous power that he refers to as "God" in his book *Kalām Cosmological Argument*, dating from the year 2000.

Craig further refined his belief in the existence of a supreme being who created the universe with intentionality in his 2009 book

Blackwell Companion to Natural Theology. Here, Craig builds upon the initial syllogism of the Kalām cosmological argument:

1. A first state of the material world cannot have a material explanation and must originate *ex nihilo* in being without material cause, because no natural explanation can be causally prior to the very existence of the natural world (space-time and its contents). It follows necessarily that the cause is outside of space and time (i.e., *timeless, spaceless, immaterial*, and *enormously powerful*) in bringing the entirety of material reality into existence.
2. Even if positing a plurality of causes prior to the origin of the universe, the causal chain must terminate in a cause which is absolutely first and *uncaused*, otherwise an infinite regress of causes would arise.
3. Occam's Razor maintains that *unicity* of the First Cause should be assumed unless there are specific reasons to believe that there is more than one causeless cause.
4. Agent causation, volitional action, is the only ontological condition in which an effect can arise in the absence of prior determining conditions. Therefore, only *personal, free agency* can account for the origin of a first temporal effect from a changeless cause.
5. Abstract objects, the only other ontological category known to have the properties of being uncaused, spaceless, timeless and immaterial, do not sit in causal relationships, nor can they exercise volitional causal power.

Craig concludes that the cause of the existence of the universe is an "uncaused, personal Creator...who *sans* the universe is beginningless, changeless, immaterial, timeless, spaceless and enormously powerful."

While Craig builds his theory on many of the latest scientific discoveries about the origins and nature of our universe, such as the Big Bang, the idea of a cosmic singularity, and Einsteinian relativity, the one aspect that is missing from Craig's rational argument, and counterarguments made by critics and skeptics of his theory, is the power and energy of love.

Love is where The One resides, an energy field beyond comprehension, one needing nothing more. The love of The One existed completely within the Trinity; there was no "Heaven" inhabited by this true God. There was no need for such, until so desired by The One, and for reasons to be revealed.

Contemplating love as the unifying energy of all creation, but which remains elusive to current rational, scientific minds, isn't all that shocking when we consider how long it took for humankind to understand gravity.

It is hard for most of us to believe it wasn't until Sir Isaac Newton published *Principia* in 1687 that gravity was finally understood to be a universal force.

The profundity of this realization/revelation can be discerned via the fact that gravity is now considered one of the four fundamental interactions of nature: gravity, electromagnetic, strong, and weak forces.

Prior to Newton, gravity had been considered a "quality." It took the application of mathematics and science to generate this critical shift of meaning from quality to force. And, ultimately, study of the force of gravity would lead Albert Einstein to his general theory of relativity and the realization of space-time curvature, new theories of cosmology, and the physical shape of the universe.

In light of gravity's historical and scientific evolution, positing a similar revelation and shift in understanding regarding love as the essential force of the universe, is neither inconceivable nor farfetched. Indeed, there is increasing hypothesizing of love as the ultimate vibrational frequency.

Some have put forth 432 Hz, 528 Hz, and/or 639 Hz as healing and "miracle" tones. Others have postulated 7.83 Hz as a curative frequency based on its association with vibrations generated by lightning discharges between Earth's surface and the ionosphere. These global electromagnetic tones are called the Schumann resonances (SR). Whether or not these are frequencies derived from The One, the salient point is that scientific discovery of love as a genuine force/ energy of the universe will at some point in time occur.

We as humans have learned a very important lesson about love: it must be shared. Love must flow forth from one Trinity to another. St. Paul has described and defined love in ways truly reflective of The One's intention. We humans, in the course of our lifetime, experience this depth of love only in rare moments, whereas love is the energy of The One.

So, if we as human beings experience love when it is directed toward another, it makes sense that the source of all love, The One, would, when so moved, share this love with an extension of itself. This is when "The One" becomes the "Creator."

THE PROGRESSION OF CREATION FROM THE ONE TO THE HEAVENLY FATHER

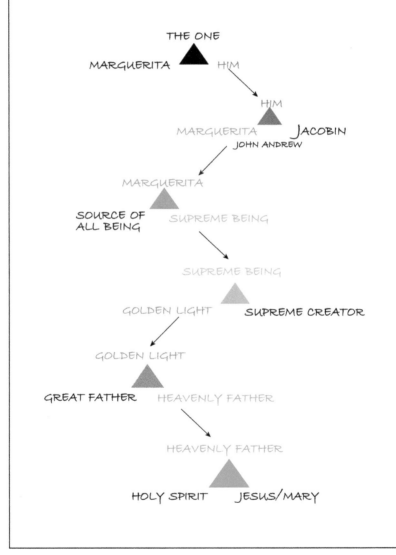

THE ONE

MARGUERITA HIM

HIM

MARGUERITA JACOBIN

JOHN ANDREW

MARGUERITA

SOURCE OF ALL BEING SUPREME BEING

SUPREME BEING

GOLDEN LIGHT SUPREME CREATOR

GOLDEN LIGHT

GREAT FATHER HEAVENLY FATHER

HEAVENLY FATHER

HOLY SPIRIT JESUS/MARY

Creation Begins

We know that all human life begins as a single cell. It takes the love of two people coming together to energize an egg. This infusion of love makes the egg complete. It commences division, a cellular multiplication according to a divine plan imprinted in DNA that forms the unique human person. This is an earthy reflection of how The One worked - and works.

A perfect analogy is that of an oyster. As odd as it might seem, imagine The One existing as the most perfect oyster. An oyster nurtured not by the sea, but by an endless source of love. A love so intense and wonderful The One captures some of it and forms it into a pearl. When that pearl is itself perfect, The One casts it forth into a universe it has created for this pearl.

Since so much of Western civilization can be traced back to the Greeks, let us use the Greek word for "pearl," Μαργαρίτης. It is from here that we derive the name: Marguerita. Hence, let us name this "pearl" the first fruit of The One: Marguerita. As the first fruit, first offspring, of The One, Marguerita exists in a symbiotic relationship with The One. They feed each other with the energy we call love. She is more than merely an extension of the Supreme Creator. We can say her soul, her innate energy, is a part of his.

It echoes Aristotle's statement that "love is composed of a single soul inhabiting two bodies." The One and Marguerita are, for all intents and purposes, a single soul inhabiting two existential supernatural entities: what we would deem "male" and "female." Marguerita, therefore, possesses incredibly powerful sources of pure energy, wisdom, and love as part of her mystical persona.

As the first fruit of The One, Marguerita shares intimately with The One's intention toward all creation: that which was and what is to be. This gift of insight into The One's intention is what we call the gift of wisdom. Marguerita's wisdom manifests as part of The One's overall intention toward everything. As such, Marguerita is the only creation and extension of The One who knows and embodies the overall Divine Plan. Marguerita's wisdom comes from knowing all and the reason for all.

Genesis confirms for us that The One relishes the act of creation; he is pleased with his creations. The glory, wonder, and love The One gifted to Marguerita spurred on the desire for further creation. As any father or mother knows, the creation of children multiplies love. Love does not run short when there are multiple children; it taps an endless source of energy, allowing a parent to love all children equally. So it was - and is - with The One.

The pearl-like perfection Marguerita manifested led The One to continue the act of procreation. This divine plan led to the creation of entities we humans refer to as "supernatural or celestial beings." To The One, however, they were works of sentient art, created for purposes deigned by The One, instrumental in the creation of what we call the universe and, perhaps, multiple universes.

We think within the parameters of human existence. Our vocabulary reflects that and, consequently, makes describing The One's handiwork difficult. Still, let us try to weave our human vocabulary and understanding with what we might call the fantastical.

The One and Marguerita dwelt in a symbiotic relationship of love flowing back and forth between them, even as The One contemplated the next acts in the Divine Plan. This Divine Plan entailed creating a cosmos, a tangible expression of its creative desire, power, and love.

Let us be clear: Marguerita is not the "wife" of The One. She is the first release of The One's love, the first labor, the first fruit, the first act of conception emanating from The One. What was born here was the first duality: The One and its extension, one with, yet distinct from, the source. The One saw and knew this was good. Love shared is love multiplied. The One, pleased beyond all knowing with Marguerita, continued the act and art of parthenogenesis.

The One desired the energy of love to possess ethereal, spiritual form. We humans know that our physical blueprint and template is contained in our DNA. DNA are molecules that carry the genetic instructions used in the growth, development, functioning, and reproduction of all known living organisms. This is an earthly reflection of what and how The One initiated creation of all that is visible and invisible.

The One ushered forth its energy of love in the form of celestial beings. They were created and charged by The One with the unfolding of the incredibly complex Divine Plan.

Perhaps the easiest way to comprehend, in human terms, the power and energy of these celestial beings is to think of the electromagnetic spectrum that defines the wavelengths and photon energies of all energy in our universe. Within the electromagnetic spectrum, we find that "light" occupies only a small portion of that continuum. Within that small vector we call light are further wavelength deviations that result in distinct colors. Hence, the effect of a prism. Each celestial being, therefore, is more akin to the overall electromagnetic spectrum, although its eminence glows as the color gold.

The One, Marguerita, and another being known as Him, from the sound of his energy, exist therefore as the original Trinity. The Trinitarian desire of The One is a self-replicating, flowing love, binding together this original Trinity in total unity, desire, and determination. This Trinitarian impetus would become the foundational pillar of all creation in the discovery of other trinities.

Within our own material realm, we see the Trinity at work in the very building block of all matter: atoms. Atoms are comprised of three tiny kinds of subatomic particles: protons, neutrons, and electrons. The protons and the neutrons make up the center of the atom called the nucleus. The electrons fly around and above the nucleus in, basically, a small orbiting cloud. We can posit the duality of protons and neutrons as the bond between The One, Marguerita and Him, while the orbiting electrons are representative of the celestial creations spawned from this original union.

Before time started, only utter darkness with a pinpoint of white life within it existed. There was no movement, no apparent life. When the blackness and speck of white life began to pulsate, a part of the white light separated from the utter darkness, leaving a smaller portion behind. The separated part, however, was still attached to it by a slim cord of creative energy.

The utter darkness is called "The One" from the sound of his energy. He is much greater than those who we have designated as God. Man created this term because no one knew what such beings should be named. Too complicated for the human mind, the beginning of life is a great mystery that will never be fully understood. The white light that left the blackness is known as Marguerita. She carried within herself two yet unknown celestial entities that would eventually be named Jacobin, and even later, their offspring, John Andrew. Both of them remained hidden until the time designated to be revealed by a divine plan. Marguerita and Jacobin were created to make life perfect.

The only way to explain what happened is that life is the first "experiment" of The One who did not want to be alone and, therefore, feel alone. To accomplish this, he had to release some of his life forces to create both "another" and other worlds within his own.

Marguerita eventually created a white circle of energy with many different energies within it. They were connected in a cluster, giving energy to one another and, thus, supporting one another. Among these energies were many gifts such as wisdom and love given to the various spiritual shapes being formed.

Although still dormant, but already in a hierarchical assembly, they became celestial beings later known as Him, the Supreme Creator, the Golden Light, the Source of All Being, the Supreme Being, and the Great Father. They would eventually become alone and apart from one another. But at this stage, they were still closely connected and shared the same energy within this white circle of light.

After a long rest, Marguerita created a thinner black circle of energy and light. Within it, these beings were separated from one another and received the creative energies they would need for the particular purposes for which they were created.

It was Marguerita who gave them their designated energy. When she activated each and brought them to full life, they began to pulsate. She drew these energies from the white speck to which she was still connected. Each being became unique and differentiated, yet they remain connected today.

The Great Father became more fully alive from the energy shared with him from each of these beings. He is still linked to all of them but, as strange as it may seem, nonetheless, stands alone. Marguerita gave him additional energy when it was time for the two of them to create various forms of life as everything unfolded according to the Divine Plan.

Of particular interest is the spiritual being released from The One. He is named Him. His role was to assist in the process of creating the heavens, the Earth, and all of creation by providing the creative energy needed. He began to pulsate when he left The One, releasing what appeared to be pockets of energy. Each was unique in size and in possessing beautiful colors to be used in creation. It was to Him that the negative energy generated on Earth would be given to be cleansed. He will also have an important role at the end of time.

These pockets of energy were used in all forms of creation, including archangels, human beings and guardian angels. Each soul would be developed from one of these bubbles that came from The One. Now their energy is needed to help sustain the universe. These small spheres of light are beginning to enter our universe once again but cannot be seen. We do not know yet for what purpose.

These celestial beings, in a unity of love, were now ready to institute the next phase of the divine plan: the creation of the universe. To do so, and to do so properly, in accordance with The One's will, yet another dynamic entity had to be spawned who would marshal these myriad energies into the creation of a true spiritual realm.

The importance of Marguerita in relation to the Great Father is in establishing the duality of "male" and "female" that would come to delineate the human race. Marguerita instilled in the Great Father a specific type of vitality that allowed him to stand alone. She was one with the core, soul, and heart of the Great Father. This vitality and energy were Marguerita's gifts of pure love. It distinguished the Great Father from the other celestial beings. Together, Marguerita and the Great Father possessed the energy necessary to create Heaven and Earth and all the forms of life to come.

So strong was the sense of purpose with which Marguerita endowed the Great Father, he believed he and Marguerita were the only sources of sentient life in the spiritual universe. Marguerita, though, was invested deeply in the Divine Plan and therefore knew of the spiritual hierarchy of celestial beings. She kept this to herself and said nothing to the Great Father.

The Great Father's charge was to oversee creation of the spiritual world formed before the physical universe we inhabit currently. This spiritual world, abounding in splendor, adorned with color, held together by the energy of divine love, would form the template for creation of the material world. Everything we see in our earthly plane of existence is a pale reflection of something that already exists in spiritual perfection.

The closest we can come to comprehending this spiritual reality would be the Greek philosopher Plato's Theory of Forms. Simply put, Plato's Theory of Forms posits that truth is to be found not in our material world but on a different plane of existence, a non-material world of ideas or forms. Plato, who existed in a pre-Christian world, tapped into an innate belief that everything we see in this material world exists as a perfect ideal reality on a spiritual plane. And the fact that we are able to imagine such, including such concepts as justice and beauty, means our souls must have known these forms before we were born. But we are getting ahead of ourselves.

So to review: in the beginning there existed The One in and of itself. Out of an abundance of love and not wanting to be alone, when so desired and deemed, The One spawned the pearl of wisdom we call Marguerita, part of, yet distinct, from The One. The energy of love that is The One was then made manifest in Him, the holder of the keys to the Divine Plan. Herein we have the original Holy Trinity, insight into The One's desire to work in Trinitarian ways.

In preparation for spiritual habitation, the Supreme Creator brought forth the Source of All Being and the Supreme Being: A veritable order of love embodied in celestial entities. Finally, in preparation for the establishment of a corporeal universe, a plane of existence marked by matter and powered by the energy of gravity and laws of physics, the Great Father welcomed the wisdom of Marguerita. As this world would be an imitation of the spiritual realm created by the energy of the Golden Light, the decision was made to create spiritual or celestial beings of less stature than the spiritual hierarchy above but endowed with the power of creation.

Here we see the wisdom, desire, and the mystery of the second Trinity. This triad of the Supreme Creator, the Golden Light, and the Great Father constitute the building blocks of the first spiritual, and then corporeal, universe we would ultimately come to inhabit.

The process of helping to create the universe that we inhabit was entrusted by the second Trinity to five supernatural entities. The closest we can come to understanding the connection and relationship between these five spiritual entities is to view them as "sons" of the Great Father and Marguerita. They were "brothers" to each other, albeit with an intrinsic hierarchy of energy; the eldest being strongest, the youngest being weakest.

We need look no further than our own material universe to see hierarchies of matter. Glancing skyward at night, our eyes are bathed in light emanating from neutron stars, black dwarfs, white dwarfs, brown dwarfs, red dwarfs, yellow dwarfs, blue giants, red giants, blue supergiants, and red supergiants. These stars are categorized by luminosity and spectral color configuration. Color indicates the chemical composition, the elemental DNA, of the star.

This is all very much a material instantiation of how The One devised a Divine Plan, then spawned sentient spirits, giving each accordingly a particular purpose.

The Great Father was unknowingly infused with energy from Marguerita and the preceding order of celestial beings. This nurturing gestation culminated in the springing forth of a new creation. As with the birth of a new star, this entity of raw energy would evolve into its own sentient spiritual being. As this new source of energy evolved, the Great Father realized that what he had brought forth was an imitation of himself. It was a firstborn son.

As with all creation, be it spiritual, artistic, or material, energy is expended and needs to be replenished. It is no different in the spiritual realm. As we hear in Genesis, acts of creation must be followed by periods of rest. How long this rest lasts remains a mystery. Who can truly define the "days" of Genesis when time as we know it did not exist? It could mean millions, billions, or trillions of "years."

In keeping with the charge of creation he had been given by The One, the Great Father upon awakening ordained that this offspring would be given part of the spiritual universe in which to create lesser spiritual beings as subjects and followers. This realm within the spiritual universe would become, in essence, his kingdom. In this kingdom lesser spiritual beings would care for the Great Father's offspring and one another. This kingdom was intended to last forever in peace.

The Great Father followed the same process in creation of three additional sons. In the same manner as the first, he entrusted each with his own designated spiritual domain as personal kingdoms. Also given were the spiritual seeds of life, what we call "souls," to inhabit each spiritual domain. It is important to remember these beings were entirely spiritual. It is only with the creation of humanity that the spiritual is eventually combined with physical, material form.

It was always necessary for the Great Father to rest and be renewed after each of these nativities, because the gestation and birthing process required so much energy. After the fourth son was born, presumably the last, Marguerita, ever a maternal presence, placed the Great Father into a much deeper, longer rest, a period of resuscitation, of restorative love.

Each of these heavenly beings is unique. They exist in a hierarchy of power and intelligence according to their birth. The eldest being the most powerful and intelligent, with a subsequent lessening of each attribute in descending order of origin. For what we would term ages, each son believed he existed solely and exclusively within his spiritual domain. Unaware of the Great Father, Marguerita, or their siblings, each believed he lived alone in his kingdom with his subjects. Only through the telling of this story have they become aware of one another and other more powerful beings in the universe.

Each of the four brothers possesses a different type of energy that makes each one unique. They are discerned individually by a specific color emanating from within, most often various shades of red and brown, colors reflecting the life forces provided by the Golden Light. These forces flowed from The One through the Supreme Creator and the Golden Light and then to each son from the Great Father and Marguerita.

None of them questioned where this energy or power came from to create their kingdoms and the subjects inhabiting it. They believed simply that the potential for new life existed within themselves. In what we might term as divine instinct, each son sensed there was an inherent, intrinsic purpose and intentionality and that each was working according to this innate, intrinsic instinct.

The four brothers do not possess free will like the Great Father, but instead they possess energy and intuition informing them of what they must do. To sustain their kingdoms, they learned how to pull powerful energies from the outer edges of the universe, in much the same way that super black holes are able to absorb entire galaxies. This is an ability that is not limited to these spiritual beings, for in the future, humankind will learn how to harness these energies as well.

Contemplating a universe overseen by multiple celestial beings, like archangels - not themselves "Gods" but rather immortal beings assigned specific spiritual (and eventually physical) domains - should not be all that surprising. How often have you looked at the night sky and pondered the vastness of our galaxy? If that isn't mind-boggling enough, try comprehending a universe of two trillion galaxies, or maybe even more. Not planetary systems, but entire galaxies, many much larger than our own Milky Way. There are more than enough for a family of immortals to oversee, to care for, to love. And, as with any extended family, there is the innate desire to contact each other, something humankind has suspected (and experienced) throughout its history. That prospect will be discussed shortly.

The coming of Michael infuriated an
already irate and jealous Lucifer.

Credit: Claudio García

Lucifer, Jesus, and Mary Come into Being

As we have just learned, the Great Father and Marguerita brought forth four offspring. And, as with human childbirth, the Great Father needed to rest after each labor. Awakening from this deserved slumber, the Great Father noticed a small amount of life-giving energy remaining from what he had used to create his four sons. This energy craved for deliverance; it began to pulsate and come alive. To the surprise of the Great Father, it was a fifth son.

The Great Father pondered whether he had misplaced energies that should have been distributed evenly to his first four sons so as to create and establish perfect spiritual balance. If that had been the case, then nothing more would have been created. The universe would have remained in perfect peace and balance forever.

The Supreme Being, for whatever reason, thought otherwise. There was most definitely a reason for the fifth son, but whether this new son would be equal to his siblings remained a question for the Great Father.

The Great Father, caring for his premature offspring, placed his fifth son into a very deep sleep so he could continue his development. To nurture him, the Great Father sought additional energy from the three antecedent celestial entities that had nurtured his own birth: Marguerita, the Supreme Creator, and the Golden Light. The Great Father also secretly drew energy from his prior offspring to strengthen this fifth son. In order to protect this fifth son, the Great Father surrounded this spiritual fetus with a very powerful protective energy, something we might refer to as lightning. It is intriguing how lightning has been attributed to spiritual beings throughout human existence.

So, of these spiritual offspring of the Great Father, the ancestry of our entire human race and its history will reside primarily with this fifth son. He will be named as, and will become, our Heavenly Father.

As the Heavenly Father was the last of the Great Father's offspring, and essentially the lesser of the sons, he required special attention from the Great Father. He knew the Heavenly Father would require external support because his energy was minimal compared to what his four brothers had received. He would not allow the Heavenly Father to exist in a weakened state.

The Great Father and Marguerita are to be considered the parents of the Heavenly Father. And, as caring, loving parents, they committed to doing as much for him as they could. Marguerita treated the Heavenly Father as a mother would, but she did not tell the Great Father what he should do to provide for him. Somehow they both understood that what had happened was indeed part of the Divine Plan. They were committed to loving the Heavenly Father as much as they did the other four sons, even if he did not develop to their same full stature.

All five of these offspring of the Great Father and Marguerita were attached spiritually to one another and, of course, their parents, though they weren't aware of this intimate relationship at that time. The Heavenly Father's attachment to the Great Father and Marguerita, however, was not as strong as his brother's connection to them. In no way, though, did that discourage the Great Father from wanting to give the Heavenly Father his own kingdom and dominion as he had given his four other sons.

Even though Marguerita had brought to life other celestial beings with her energy, she did so sparingly and with great caution. Marguerita's energy was so powerful, so much a part of The One, the very source of existence, that it could potentially overcome and suffocate these spiritual offspring. She exhibited this caution even with the Golden Light. Despite this understanding, Marguerita did give a large amount of her energy to the Heavenly Father because he had received far less than his brothers. She had personal knowledge of the Divine Plan and, therefore, of what she should and should not do. She knew their fifth son, our Heavenly Father, was by no means a mistake.

Unlike his brothers, the Heavenly Father had the same spiritual form as the Great Father. They shared a snow-white brilliant energy, but the Great Father knew intrinsically that his fifth son was different than the other four. Unlike his brothers, the Great Father knew the youthful, still developing Heavenly Father would be unable to sustain and nurture a planet and its seeds of life the way his four brothers were able. The Great Father, therefore, needed to gift the Heavenly Father with a different kind of kingdom.

The first four offspring of the Great Father were able to exist on their own. Our Heavenly Father, though, needed further nourishment. It came in the form of the same energy the Golden Light had given to the Source of All Being and the Supreme Being. This very powerful celestial energy helped the Great Father promote the development of his fifth son by selecting a place in the universe where the Heavenly Father could reside and later reign independently, like his brothers, but separate from them.

To watch over and care for his fifth son, the Great Father, with the assistance and shared energy of Marguerita, created three bands of powerful spiritual beings, to be called the Angels of the Most High, to surround and sustain the life forces of the Heavenly Father. We know these powerful spiritual beings by the name of "archangels." Ironically, this arrangement would prove insufficient because there wasn't a proper balance between the Heavenly Father and these archangels.

The energy of love between Marguerita and the Great Father continued to grow and abound. Their shared love enabled them to create this archangelic source of energy to provide both balance and continuous energy to the Heavenly Father. The Heavenly Father would name his new source of life energy Lucifer as he was the first son given to him by the Great Father. Two other archangels to serve as "sons," however, would soon follow.

Lucifer's purpose was the care and sustenance of the Heavenly Father. He was an offspring, the very child, of Marguerita. In maintaining the balance ordered by the Supreme Creator, the female part of Lucifer would come to be known as Mother Nature, as real and sentient a spiritual being as Lucifer and one who would come to play a major role on both spiritual and physical Earth.

When it was time for Lucifer to be presented to the Heavenly Father, to fulfill the mission for which Lucifer was created, Marguerita and the Great Father covered him with an energy force that would look to us like a shell or blanket. This energy cocoon was necessary because Lucifer required additional time and protection before he could develop fully.

In many respects, Lucifer could be considered the sixth offspring of the Great Father and Marguerita. He was created to be a source of balance and omnipresent energy for the Heavenly Father, beyond our comprehension of either "son" or "brother," but truly first among the rank of archangels at that time.

The second of these three archangels would come to be known later by the holy and sacred name of Jesus. And, since the Supreme Creator had ordained from the beginning of all life that balance must be maintained among his creations, the female side of the archangel Jesus would come to be known as Mary. This was reflective of the duality that marked the combination of the Great Father and Marguerita, essentially the parents of the five sons and the creators of archangels.

Marguerita is truly the mother of the universe, the female half of the Great Father's paternal form. Unknown to all at this same time, there was gestating within Marguerita yet another supernatural being who would come to be called Jacobin. Jacobin is destined for the dramatic culmination to Earth's existence, according to the Divine Plan. He is of extreme importance. So much so that the energy used in his creation came directly from The One. Marguerita knew that Jacobin was more important than both the Heavenly Father and Lucifer. Consequently, she nurtured him with some of her own, more powerful, pure divine energy. At this stage of his development, however, even the Great Father did not know of Jacobin's incubation.

The needs of the fifth son were great, greater than the energy Marguerita alone was able to channel to Lucifer, as her own energy had been depleted by nurturing the others. There developed therefore a symbiotic relationship between the archangel Lucifer and the gestating Jacobin. This sharing of energy established an unknown yet tangible bond of brotherhood between Lucifer and Jacobin as both were gestated and nurtured continuously within Marguerita. Jacobin slept longer than Lucifer within Marguerita precisely because the Divine Plan called for Jacobin to experience incarnation. He would be coming to Earth as a human soul together with Marguerita.

Jacobin was so powerful that when he and Lucifer were separated, Lucifer would need to have his life force renewed constantly while Jacobin possessed within himself all the life force he would ever need. The gestating spirit of Jacobin was so prescient that while still in Marguerita's womb Jacobin knew one of his kind would instigate upheaval in the spiritual realm and that he would be charged ultimately with its resolution. He just didn't know who would incite this disorder.

According to the Divine Plan of The One, it will be Jacobin - and he alone - who will sever completely Lucifer's life forces still connected to the Heavenly Father when life on Earth is ended. Before that climactic confrontation occurs, however, Jacobin will undergo a further transformation and will become known by the name of Michael the Archangel. But we are getting ahead of ourselves.

Lucifer was created primarily with energy from Marguerita and the Great Father. This energy, though, was different from that with which she had nurtured Jacobin. Still, Lucifer was more beautiful and appeared to be more powerful than any other celestial being, including the archangels Jesus and Jacobin. Lucifer possessed incredible strength from the energies channeled his way from so many powerful supernatural forces, power passed on to him from the Great Father and Marguerita. Lucifer was the image of the perfect archangel, but his identity was becoming more powerful than it should have been. He did this by using for himself energy that was destined for the care and sustenance of the Heavenly Father.

Lucifer's role was to provide the pure energy of love to the Heavenly Father, caring for and sustaining him while he rested, regained, and then maintained his intrinsic equilibrium. Retaining energy intended for the Heavenly Father eventually put Lucifer and the Heavenly Father seriously out of balance. This imbalance would have serious implications. According to the Divine Plan, neither of them should have received such quantities of energy. This energy is love, but love cannot always place limits on itself. Love believes it knows what is best and gives as much as it can without considering the consequences.

We need rightfully ask: where was all this activity taking place? This requires important clarification. Heaven, as we know it now, did not yet exist as a dwelling place within the universal spectrum of existence. Everything we have spoken of so far existed within a celestial sphere, essentially a meta-heaven. Heaven, as we know it today, and this primordial celestial sphere are separate and distinct from one another. Our heaven would be created later, albeit within this celestial realm, during a time of great conflict.

The Heavenly Father was excited when Lucifer appeared. He did not know from where he had come, but an intimate bond of love developed immediately. In his great excitement, he couldn't wait to open the spiritual shell covering Lucifer. Joy overwhelmed him such that he could not delay his coming forth. His great desire to see what was inside this miraculous cocoon was the beginning of what humankind would come to know as curiosity.

The Heavenly Father, however, should not have opened Lucifer's protective covering when he did. Though motivated by love, the Heavenly Father's action would essentially cause Lucifer to be born prematurely. More energy should have been given to help Lucifer achieve his full maturation, but it was stunted when he was taken out of his shell too soon. According to the Divine Plan, however, Lucifer was not supposed to grow to full stature - for reasons we will soon learn.

At this time the Heavenly Father considered himself to be a solitary spiritual being, alone within the celestial realm. This supernatural solipsism was identical in outlook to his four other brothers of whom he was not yet aware. His sovereign domain consisted entirely of himself and Lucifer. The energy he received unknowingly from the pantheon of other celestial beings gave him great power, though no greater than the power given to his four brothers. This energy and spiritual comportment made him like a God.

He could only conclude, therefore, that Lucifer had come forth from his own being. In his way of thinking, all that mattered was that he now had an external entity that would care for him, one who would cover him with a blanket of loving energy to comfort him when he needed to rest.

Lucifer would eventually reject the role assigned to him by the Great Father and Marguerita to care for the Heavenly Father. The great tragedy was that Lucifer never fully comprehended just how much the Heavenly Father loved him. He still doesn't.

Like the Heavenly Father, Lucifer had to rest occasionally in order to regenerate and renew his life force. As our physical world was created, Lucifer sought out and absorbed energy from our planetary formation, even energy from our moon. At first this energy was smooth and comforting to him. It was a beautiful white color. In time it transitioned to gray, finally devolving into black. By then it was no longer a comfort to him. This is why angels created later would venerate Lucifer as the "God of Darkness." It was a name he gave to himself.

Lucifer carried out his responsibility to sustain the Heavenly Father faithfully for countless eons. During the course of this servitude, however, Lucifer would very slowly grow jealous of the Heavenly Father. This encroaching jealousy would motivate Lucifer to do what was strictly forbidden: he began to draw ever increasing amounts of pure loving energy from the Heavenly Father unto himself. He did this while the Heavenly Father rested in dormancy, seeking renewal of energy. Furthermore, Lucifer began to plot how he could become stronger than the Heavenly Father, eventually overtake him and rule their shared domain. His scheming involved befriending other angelic beings so they would serve him in the same way Lucifer had been charged with serving the Heavenly Father.

When the Heavenly Father realized what Lucifer was conspiring, he was both disappointed and concerned but he loved Lucifer so much that he chose not to stop him. Instead, he would frequently and quickly forgive Lucifer for what the Heavenly Father believed was merely a minor weakness, one that could and would be corrected. He believed Lucifer would change. It was to be an unfulfilled prelude to the story of the Prodigal Son.

This unfolding of unfortunate events began with the premature birth of Lucifer. When we say Lucifer had not formed fully, we mean Lucifer failed to achieve energy balance. As humans, we see this as an equilibrium between male and female energies. The Heavenly Father should have realized there was a problem when Lucifer emerged from his womb and arrogantly shoved aside his feminine energy.

This energy took on spiritual form and become known to us as Mother Nature. Lucifer rejected her when she began to assume responsibilities specifically given to her by the Great Father and Marguerita. Lucifer's personality was immature, afflicted with selfishness and jealousy, and he was threatened by discovering a fellow spiritual being who he feared might eventually overtake him. Ironically, Mother Nature was the weaker of them both at that time, but Lucifer did not realize that yet.

The archangels have a special energy force that reflects the purpose for which that particular collection of archangels was created. They each have different wavelengths of energy, though oftentimes indistinguishable from each other. Lucifer and Mother Nature were created to work together via symbiotic life-sustaining energy. This ongoing exchange, if it had been maintained, would have enabled them to remain in balance and therefore fully "alive."

Mother Nature was not exempt from this same egotistic drive. She wanted to be as independent and dominant as Lucifer. The premature opening and closing of the celestial womb affected her development as well.

Lucifer desired to rule the universe, but he was afraid Mother Nature would try to take away some of his energy. He even feared her aspiring dominance. So he hid himself from her. Lucifer and Mother Nature have always been, and still are, at odds with one another, even though they both sprang from the same life source.

This is why Mother Nature will always be connected loosely to Lucifer. It also explains why she can become erratic at times. Biblical disasters like the Great Flood were the result of her pent-up anger against both Lucifer and the nascent human race who were destroying much of the Earth she had created with the Heavenly Father. Her great anger still expresses itself via prodigious natural disasters. She does this in the hope that such calamity will bring us ever closer to the Heavenly Father. Unfortunately, it usually has the opposite effect, with people questioning why the Heavenly Father allows such natural death and destruction to occur.

When Lucifer cast Mother Nature aside, she cried out in prophetic warning, "In time, Lucifer, your words will destroy you." He did not understand what she meant, did not know how to respond, and, consequently, chose to ignore her. These warning words though will remain with him until the end of time. When Lucifer and Mother Nature quarrel, one or both of them play havoc with Earth's weather, causing great death and destruction on the Earth.

Lucifer tries to use this devastation to his advantage by proclaiming to hurt and injured humanity, "See, your Heavenly Father doesn't answer your prayers." Though humanity does not actually hear this admonition, the ethos becomes embedded in its psyche, further disparaging the Heavenly Father. This is yet one more reason why Lucifer will be cut off from the celestial plane at the end of time.

Lucifer enjoys taunting the Heavenly Father, knowing that each assault causes the Heavenly Father sadness and saps him of energy. This antagonism will continue until the end of time. The Supreme Creator, the Golden Light, and the Great Father are fully aware of what Lucifer is doing, but they are loath to intervene as it is all part of the Divine Plan.

The Great Father wants to end this vicious antipathy, but he is powerless to do so because it was he who created Lucifer as a life source for the Heavenly Father. If allowed, the Great Father would cut the life cord between Lucifer and the Heavenly Father. Doing so, however, would abrogate the Divine Plan; and so he is not allowed to intervene directly.

The Great Father, knowing he had to do something to address the serious imbalance between Lucifer and the Heavenly Father, would undertake a drastic measure ultimately affecting all humanity. The Great Father appropriated one of the archangels surrounding the Heavenly Father and positioned him alongside Lucifer.

This chosen archangel was Jesus.

In his new role, Jesus would act like a second son to the Heavenly Father, providing him with the vital life forces needed for regeneration. This was the Great Father's way of indirectly preparing Lucifer for his eventual separation from the Heavenly Father and the celestial realm. It also triggered the antipathy that would come to exist between Lucifer and Jesus, both in Heaven and on the Earth.

It is impossible to speak of Jesus the Archangel without recognizing Mary as part of him. What we refer to as "male" and "female" energies are present in all archangels. And this energy comes ultimately from The One through Marguerita and into all creation. Jesus and Mary therefore, in the form of a single archangel, supported one another, grew ever closer, and formed a perfect balance.

Lucifer despised the archangel Jesus/Mary from their first manifestation. When Lucifer began to steal life-sustaining forces from the Heavenly Father, he tried to win over the other archangels being created for the Heavenly Father by sharing this stolen energy with them. It was bribery in its earliest form.

Lucifer's hope was that this same group of archangels would surround him when he finally overpowered the Heavenly Father and became ruler of the universe. Some archangels, especially Jesus/Mary, refused to accept the energy offered by Lucifer. They remained loyal and true to the purpose for which they were created. This aroused the anger, animosity, and fury of Lucifer.

Lucifer feared that Jesus/Mary might become too close to the Heavenly Father and in so doing discover Lucifer's nefarious intentions. As the first of the archangels, Lucifer had the power to refuse acceptance and divert Jesus's energy away from the Heavenly Father. He feared that by allowing Jesus's energy to renew the Heavenly Father this would thwart his takeover plans.

All Jesus/Mary could do then was direct their loving energy toward the Heavenly Father, hoping he would find a way to become aware of it and retrieve it. Lucifer, though, had the power to negate this intention. As the first son of the Heavenly Father, it had been established that all life-sustaining energy had to pass through him before it could be given to the Heavenly Father.

The mother of all archangels is Marguerita; the paternal force is the Great Father. To recount, Lucifer and Jacobin were formed together in the womb of Marguerita at the same time. They were not identical twins, but rather fraternal twins. The seeds for all archangels gestated within Marguerita. She had the strength to do incredible things, but she did not have the power to create archangels all by herself. She needed the help of the Great Father. He could provide Marguerita not only with his own loving energy, but also energy taken from his four other sons. It was the combined energy of the Great Father and Marguerita that would produce these archangelic offspring.

After Lucifer and Jesus/Mary, Jacobin, the nascent child of Marguerita, became the third archangel given to the Heavenly Father by the Great Father. He too was given the purpose of providing life-sustaining energy to the Heavenly Father.

When the Great Father became aware of Jacobin's presence within the womb of Marguerita, alongside that of Lucifer, he moved to keep the two separate, distinct, and unknown to each other. Jacobin, while unexpected, exuded tremendous potential, such that the Great Father feared Jacobin might not be able to control the great energy provided to him by Marguerita. The Great Father feared an unleashed Jacobin might be able to destroy both the Heavenly Father and Lucifer. He could not, and would not, allow this to happen. As it turns out this fear was unwarranted, but only Marguerita knew the true intentions of the Divine Plan and how it would prevent such a conflagration from occurring.

The seed of Jacobin had been part of Marguerita from the time of her own birth from The One. When the seed of Jacobin became sentient, he looked with wonder and bewilderment at both the Great Father and Marguerita. The Marguerita who Jacobin first saw appeared mysterious and unknown. She was drawn, exhausted, and appeared nearly lifeless due to the strenuous labor of delivering Lucifer, Jacobin, and the host of celestial beings. Even in this depleted state, though, Marguerita remained far more powerful than any other being.

The maternal bond between child and mother began to take hold between Jacobin and Marguerita. He became very sensitive and caring toward this withered entity. Not fully knowing why, Jacobin realized that it was now his turn to nurture Marguerita. In an expression of great love, he began to share the energy that had been implanted and imparted to him by Marguerita with her. Child was now nurturing mother.

This natal cycle completed, it was now time for Marguerita to separate from the Great Father. This was all part of the Divine Plan. The energy hidden within Marguerita remained very strong, even after delivering Jacobin and Lucifer. The combined energies of Marguerita and Jacobin, however, were beyond daunting. So much so that the Great Father feared for his own existence. In many respects he was correct, for the combined power of Marguerita and Jacobin would be greater than the Heavenly Father, and perhaps even more than the Supreme Creator. And rightly so, because this dynamic energy would be needed as the Divine Plan unfolded. In accordance with this destiny, upon separation from the Great Father, Jacobin would henceforth be known as Michael the Archangel.

Despite this well-spring of energy and ascension among the rank of archangels and despite recognition as the third son of the Heavenly Father, Michael was no more successful than Jesus/Mary in imparting energy to the Heavenly Father. Like Jesus/Mary, Michael could only place his energy force near the Heavenly Father. Single-minded, nefarious Lucifer continued to block its infusion.

The coming of Michael infuriated an already irate and jealous Lucifer. He hated Michael and Marguerita even more than he did Jesus/Mary. This fervent animosity concerned the Heavenly Father. It even aroused suspicion about Jesus/Mary and Jacobin from the Heavenly Father himself whose foremost concern was maintaining what he still believed to be a sincere loving relationship between him and Lucifer.

As one can easily deduce, the situation in the celestial realm was rife with conflict, suspicion, animosity, and outright hatred. The more energy Jesus/Mary and Michael tried to provide to the Heavenly Father, the more energy Lucifer siphoned away - and the stronger he became. The positive news is that much of this loving energy given by Jesus/Mary and Michael to the Heavenly Father remains near him to this day

As he fell from heaven, Lucifer let out a scream
that caused fault lines to form on Earth.

The Celestial Realm
Is Rent Asunder

Lucifer and Michael were, and still are, the same yet different. They were two incredibly powerful and beautiful archangels sharing the same basic source of energy, albeit with one important exception: Michael received his energy directly from The One; Lucifer received only some of that same energy albeit indirectly from Marguerita.

If Lucifer could have destroyed Jesus and Michael, he would have done so immediately and without any hesitation. Marguerita, however, enshrouded both Jesus and Michael with a spiritual barrier of loving energy to protect and shield them both from Lucifer.

At Michael's birth, but before he was given to the Heavenly Father as a third child, he was placed immediately in repose by Marguerita within the Great Father. This allowed Michael further development. Taking energy from the Great Father, Michael continued to develop his strength. This was in sharp distinction to Lucifer who continued to drain energy intended for the Heavenly Father.

Not all energy is alike. Energy from the Great Father is more powerful than energy from the Heavenly Father. Consequently, Michael is endowed with the vitality that will allow him to prevail ultimately in his battle with Lucifer at the end of time. But again, we are getting ahead of ourselves.

Paths taken by both Lucifer and Michael paralleled their distinct responsibilities: the same time Lucifer was drawing close to the Heavenly Father, Michael was growing closer to the Great Father. They were indeed brothers, though neither Lucifer nor Michael realized it at that time. More importantly, Lucifer didn't understand what role Michael would play in his life. With the telling of this story, it has been revealed to him at last. His curiosity and concern have been piqued. This news is of such a shock to him that he refuses to believe it. Yet it is absolutely true.

We can attribute this to Lucifer's egotism. And we can attribute this egotism to a megalomania caused by Lucifer overindulging, and ultimately overdosing, on the loving energy intended for the Heavenly Father. As he gorged himself on the Heavenly Father's energy, Lucifer developed an overwhelming desire for ever more power and control. Love intended for the Heavenly Father became turned inward. It became self-love. What he thought would be an unending fountain of goodness and affirmation wound up doing him more harm than good.

It is necessary to state outright: if Lucifer had remained faithful to the role in which he had been created, it would have been the final stage of creation. The spiritual realm would have been in perfect balance. There would have been no dissension in the celestial realm, nor any need for humanity. Peace and love would rule throughout the celestial realm and eternity. Alas, that was not part of the Divine Plan.

In fact, Lucifer would have been given an even more important role in the spiritual universe. Power and greed, however, blinded him. These negative traits turned him into what he is now: the source of every form of evil throughout the universe. Perhaps even more damning is that Lucifer brought forth death. We can call death "Lucifer's curse." Death originally was to be seen as an event of great blessing, love, and spiritual renewal. It still can be, as we will soon learn.

The act of sharing love energy between the Heavenly Father and Lucifer had a side benefit of which neither was aware. The fraternal bond between Lucifer and Michael allowed for a portion of this divine energy to be siphoned off to Michael. Marguerita was secretly taking a portion of this same energy away from Lucifer and giving it to Michael. Michael would cleanse this energy of Lucifer's ill intent, return it to his mother, who in turn would channel it to the Heavenly Father. Consider it a supernatural conspiracy: the ultimate goal being to sustain the life source of the Heavenly Father without Lucifer's knowledge.

As Lucifer grew ever more jealous of the Heavenly Father and gave vent to his ego via disobedience of his created purpose, the nature of his energy began to change. No longer did it exude life-sustaining energy but instead took on a destructive inclination. When Lucifer discovered the capabilities this newfound energy provided, he began to cover the Heavenly Father with it. It was Lucifer's way of gradually weakening and, ultimately, binding the Heavenly Father.

The positive life forces of the Heavenly Father began to diminish from this corona of negativity. Consequently, the Heavenly Father needed to rest ever more frequently and for much longer periods of time. Without realizing it, the Heavenly Father could be said to have started a process of dying.

This was precisely Lucifer's wish and intent. As his own strength increased and the Heavenly Father's decreased, Lucifer's lust for power intensified. His ego turned into pure avarice: he now wanted all of the Heavenly Father's life force and total control of his celestial realm. And things seemed to be going exactly as he had planned.

Knowing this imbalance was wrecking the peace and sanctity of the spiritual dominion, the Great Father decided it was time to expel Lucifer from the celestial realm. Urged on by Marguerita, the Great Father was made aware that Lucifer had developed means of fooling the Heavenly Father into believing Lucifer was only looking out for his well-being. Lucifer had essentially enveloped the Heavenly Father in a cloak of lies that hid his true maniacal intent. Lucifer was poisoning the Heavenly Father. The Heavenly Father unknowingly drank of this potion thinking it was pure love.

The Great Father and Marguerita decided Lucifer had to go. The development of his ego and self-aggrandizement threatened the balance of the celestial realm. Overturning the Divine Plan of The One, as Lucifer was doing, was unallowable and had to be stopped. The Great Father and Marguerita had to act with great urgency because Lucifer had already absconded with three-fourths of the Heavenly Father's energy. The more the Heavenly Father rested, the weaker he became—and the more determined and committed Lucifer became in his vaunted conspiracy.

The question confronting the Great Father and Marguerita, though, was this: how to effect great change in the Divine Plan without upsetting the balance of the spiritual realm. It is important to keep in mind that at this stage in the evolution of the spiritual realm, our Heavenly Father did not know of the existence of the Great Father. In the same way that we understand our universe to be so vast as to be incomprehensible, so it is in the spiritual realm. The Heavenly Father thought that he and his angelic companions were the only existing sentient beings. Much like how we humans have thought to date of our own earthly existence as unique within the galaxy and perhaps even within the universe.

The Great Father therefore set about instilling in the Heavenly Father thoughts he would comprehend as his own ideas. This is what we would call the power of unconscious suggestion. The Great Father made the Heavenly Father believe that Lucifer should have his own kingdom, that he should reign over a spiritual world in the same way the Heavenly Father's four brothers had such domains.

In anticipation of this pending separation, the Great Father had begun to design Earth as Lucifer's future kingdom. He even placed an image of what it should look like in the Heavenly Father's mind. The Great Father instilled in the Heavenly Father the belief that Lucifer would thrive in this new domain. He could be as powerful as he wanted to be. He even planted the thought that Jesus and Michael would accept Lucifer as their divine leader, feed him energy, and that this kingdom would become a utopia under Lucifer's leadership.

Lucifer's infusion of powerful energy fueled his conspiratorial thinking. As with many leaders who go mad, Lucifer sensed something was about to happen to him. It was the beginning of paranoia. Figuring the best defense was a good offense, Lucifer commenced enlisting others in his conspiratorial design. Those "others" were the band of archangels surrounding the Heavenly Father. Lucifer tempted them with the ultimate enticement: power. Lucifer promised he would give them power like his own if they were faithful to him.

Such boasting and depravity immediately unsettled the already teetering celestial balance. A great rumble occurred throughout the spiritual realm. Mother Nature heard it and knew something terrible had happened. She had been helping the Heavenly Father design this new domain called Earth for Lucifer's dominion. Even though Mother Nature was in the midst of working on his own behalf, as she was in actuality part of him, Lucifer intervened and silenced her with slumber. He would from here on out hate her for this attempted intervention, even though in so doing he was hating himself.

Mother Nature possesses the same tempestuous nature as her Luciferian side. When a second rumble occurred throughout the spiritual realm, she awakened and confronted her other half.

Mother Nature warned Lucifer that his conspiracy to overthrow the Heavenly Father was doomed to failure. She warned he was treading precariously and risked not only failing in his usurping the Heavenly Father, but with losing much of his own power. And, with losing this power, he teetered on becoming grotesque, ugly, filled with darkness. She revolted at this fratricidal intent, the stifling of her own work and purposefulness, all of which was for his benefit.

Yet she refrained from alerting the Heavenly Father to her other half's conspiracy. Her reluctance and inability may have been due to the weakened and troubled state Lucifer had forced upon her.

The internal strife between Lucifer and Mother Nature may be why they seemed preoccupied and stunned when the separation finally occurred. It happened in a split second and was the work of the Great Father and Marguerita, aided by a host of other celestial entities.

Lucifer became aware suddenly of the unfolding drama. As the spiritual surface began to sink beneath him, he rushed toward the Heavenly Father. Enraged, screaming as loudly as he could, he realized he was falling. As the Heavenly Father and the celestial realm receded from sight, Lucifer let out a vicious scream. So potent and powerful was this cry of rage it caused fault lines to form over his kingdom of Earth. That is why Earth today is volatile and unstable. There is a direct line from Lucifer's formidable irate fury to Earth's tectonic, tidal, and volcanic destruction.

In a flash Lucifer awakened on Earth, a world very distinct from what he had known before. To his shock and astonishment, he discovered he was alone. A great sadness enveloped him, much to the chagrin of the Heavenly Father, who had expected Lucifer to welcome his new realm with overwhelming joy.

His separation from the Heavenly Father, however, was neither total nor complete. Recognizing the love that had existed between Lucifer and the Heavenly Father, the Great Father and Marguerita allowed there to remain two silvery cords connecting them, albeit loosely. One connection provided Lucifer with minimal energy from the Heavenly Father, energy destined for Lucifer to use in his new kingdom as he so pleased and for as long as time existed. The second thin cord enabled communication to transpire between the Heavenly Father and his rebellious charge. Communication was scarce, minimal, and fleeting, but the connection remains.

Despite her efforts at salvaging his heavenly connection, Marguerita found humor in Lucifer's plight. She let out a laugh that remains forever in Lucifer's mind as a belittling slur, resonating with triumph and glee over him, a veritable gloating. Because of this, Lucifer hates all laughter. Even though she gave him life, Lucifer despises Marguerita, creating the first and most powerful love-hate relationship between mother and child.

This traumatic scene unfolded before Mother Nature's eyes, but she was then blessed with loss of memory. Mother Nature's silencing and Lucifer's separation, allowed Michael, who was also cut from heaven at the same time as Lucifer, to remain unseen. It was the Great Father who ordained that Michael was to be separated from the spiritual realm simultaneous with Lucifer. This had to be so according to the Divine Plan. It did not, however, reconcile for Michael the shock of this separation. He did not believe he had done anything wrong to warrant this separation. As he too fell to Earth, he sensed a need to spread his own energy over the Earth.

Even though Michael and Lucifer were expelled from the spiritual realm simultaneously, neither was aware of the other. This is both surprising yet entirely understandable. That is because Lucifer and Michael are so alike. It is akin to twins looking at each other in a mirror. Each sees the other but recognizes only himself. They are so alike that Michael and Lucifer even sound similar. The Heavenly Father sent Michael with Lucifer to Earth with the intention of them becoming partners.

If Lucifer had known Michael had fallen alongside him, he would have set out at once to annihilate him on the spot. Fortunately, Lucifer was too enraged and furious to desire anything other than revenge against the Heavenly Father, even though it was the Great Father and Marguerita who had orchestrated this separation. He was also unaware that during this great fall, Lucifer and Michael's remaining cords to the Heavenly Father became entwined. This would unite Michael and Lucifer even more. Lucifer began to receive positive energy from Michael's fountainhead, while Michael became infected with the negativity of Lucifer. Consequently, Lucifer began to deeply desire the same love for Marguerita that Michael possessed, while Michael experienced a lust for power and domination, the hallmarks of Lucifer.

The Divine Plan ordained that Michael was to live many lives on Earth. Each existence aimed at providing him the knowledge, awareness, and preparation for the culminating battle with Lucifer at Earth's end. Michael's ability to do this is a direct result of what occurred during the fall.

During the cataclysm that was the great fall from the spiritual realm, a drop of Lucifer's energy or "blood" fell on Michael. In so doing, it transformed him forever. Michael lost all feeling. This had to happen because this lack of feeling serves as protection for Michael. Because of this insulation, Lucifer is unable to find Michael during his earthly human sojourns. Lucifer sees only himself and his own lack of feeling. These markings and attributes are indelible. They will mark and remain with both of them until the end of time.

Recovering quickly from the trauma of separation, Lucifer desired to return to the celestial realm at once in hope of persuading even more angels to follow him. Again, he offered to share some of his own energy with them so long as they would show obedience to him. In the chaos of the moment, Lucifer succeeded in luring away additional archangels. A pyrrhic victory, but a small triumph nonetheless.

Lucifer is only now realizing, with the telling of this story, that some of his power comes from the Great Father, his four brothers, Marguerita, the celestial beings, and, of course, the Heavenly Father. This makes him tremendously powerful. Yet much of this power remains dormant because he has been barred the process of spiritual renewal ordained by the Heavenly Father. Ironically, only Marguerita, the spirit he despises, can renew and release the full power of Lucifer; but she never will.

Lucifer's rage has a reddish glow and looks very much like human blood. The color red also marks the eyes of Lucifer. Red symbolizes his power. Think of the atheistic revolutionary movements throughout human history and how red has so often marked the color of their flags: socialism, Nazism, communism. Human souls must pass through this veil of red energy each time they enter Earth.

Since Earth is Lucifer's kingdom until it is destroyed, all humans are touched and marked by Lucifer's energy. It is his proclamation that we belong to him. That is why Christian baptism is so important. Baptism covers Lucifer's negative energy with the positive energy of Christ. It does not completely remove it, but it does cover it and identifies us as belonging to Jesus and Mary.

Lucifer is never satisfied. He is driven entirely by the desire to rule the heavens. This kingdom of Earth did not excite him. He was further outraged upon realizing the Heavenly Father expected Lucifer to care for the children, the souls who are sharing in the life of the Heavenly Father, destined to inhabit Earth. It is this energy that sustains them. The universe was what he wanted, not a planet with human beings and other lesser forms of life. Despite being cut from the celestial realm, Lucifer still believes he is all-powerful. He wanted to get back to heaven and did not care if the Earth was destroyed in the process.

After Michael was forcibly removed from the spiritual realm but before he touched Earth, Marguerita caught and returned him to the celestial realm. She did this for the express purpose of covering him with a cloak of energy that rendered him invisible. Neither the Heavenly Father nor Lucifer knew Michael had returned. Marguerita did this because she feared Lucifer might corrupt him on Earth or, more importantly, that battle between them would commence before the designated time.

When Marguerita and Michael crossed back into the celestial realm, a very powerful energy force was expelled from within them. This blast created a second group of three bands of angelic beings called the "Archangels of the Most High." Their responsibility is to prevent Lucifer from reentering the celestial realm.

This supernova of spiritual energy also created the tangible, chosen place of existence we humans call "Heaven." The Archangels of the Most High serve as the Gates of Heaven.

Despite the presence of these very powerful archangels and because of their familial relationship, Lucifer was convinced the Heavenly Father would eventually allow him back into the celestial realm. Lucifer's appeals were heard by the Heavenly Father, but because of his weakened condition, he could not see his firstborn son. No matter how hard Lucifer tried to return to the celestial realm, his return was barred by the Archangels of the Most High. When Lucifer realized it was Marguerita who had created the Archangels of the Most High that now barred his heavenly return and had closed the "gates" of heaven, he was further enraged.

Awakening from his weakened state, the Heavenly Father was stunned to find Jesus replacing Lucifer as the source of life-giving love and energy. In this shock of sudden recognition, the Heavenly Father became angry, even though Jesus and Michael were his sons as well. He became convinced that Jesus and Michael were somehow responsible for the loss of Lucifer. The fact that Jesus was now the giver of life-sustaining energy to the Heavenly Father failed to resonate. The Heavenly Father felt profound sorrow at losing Lucifer.

Absorbing these profound changes to his spiritual kingdom, the Heavenly Father expressed genuine trepidation for how Lucifer might react to the news that Jesus had taken over his original energy-giving responsibility. Those anxieties would become a reality when the incarnate Jesus would shed his blood on the cross, counteracting the blood Lucifer spread upon the Earth when he was expelled from the celestial realm.

Lucifer's separation from the celestial realm and his arrival on young Earth signified a drastic alteration of the spiritual hierarchy. It was Michael who declared the finality of this alteration by renaming Lucifer. From this moment forward, he would be called Satan. This name negated the title of "Light Bearer" and removed any claim by Lucifer as savior or saint. He had willingly changed into something he was never ordained to be: a source of acrimony and hatred toward the Heavenly Father he was originally meant to serve.

Lucifer's appearance on the Earth was welcomed only by its serpents. The other creatures inhabiting the earth shunned him. The angels who accompanied Lucifer to his new earthly kingdom recalled how the Heavenly Father had lovingly referred to Lucifer as "God of Darkness" because Lucifer cared for the Heavenly Father while he rested. Henceforth, this once loving title would forever symbolize destruction and deceit as Lucifer reigned formally on Earth as the God of Darkness. These fallen angels would now serve and worship Lucifer, as they had once been loyal to the Heavenly Father.

Four very powerful Archangels of the Most High, ones who had admired Lucifer's beauty, position, and power, followed him almost immediately to his new kingdom on Earth. They were from the band of archangels closest to the Heavenly Father. As such, their betrayal was hurtful and shocking. They loved the Heavenly Father but did so, like Lucifer, only out of self-interest. They believed that even though Lucifer had been expelled from the celestial realm, his connection and relationship to the Heavenly Father would always remain. Their loyalty to fallen Lucifer was motivated by both jealousy and awe, recognizing the immense power he had obtained at the Heavenly Father's expense. Think how often in human history demagogues and tyrants have garnered millions of followers, even among those who inwardly despised them but who do so out of jealousy, greed, and fear.

Nearly three-fourths of the angelic hosts followed Lucifer to his new kingdom on Earth. This exodus of angels occurred over millions of our years. These angels reasoned incorrectly that the energy to create Earth, Lucifer's new kingdom, had come from the Heavenly Father who loved him greatly. They were unaware of the tremendous and important role Marguerita, the Great Father, and Mother Nature played in Earth's formation.

When they appeared on Earth, what they found, though, was a Lucifer engorged on the energy he had siphoned from the Heavenly Father. In his satiated state, Lucifer slipped into a comatose torpor for seven long periods of time. He was the supernatural version of the python who devours an animal but then needs to rest for weeks. Unknowingly, Lucifer had by his gluttony significantly weakened his own kingdom that was out of balance from its very beginning.

Those angels who followed Lucifer to Earth were shocked by their new realm. Earth's harsh atmosphere was not what these spiritual beings were accustomed to, and the result was disorientation and disillusionment. In the face of this harsh atmosphere and its harmful effects, these archangels were sucked into deep spiritual holes already existing all over primordial Earth. Unknown to these angels, these deep holes, known as "vortexes," had been shaped by the Heavenly Father's four brothers as part of the Divine Plan in concern for their brother. They had intended these vortexes to be powerful energy sources strengthening and stabilizing young Earth. They did this because Earth had been created too quickly, such that it was unfinished and unready for Lucifer's arrival.

Vortexes are places of deep mystery. Shaped like geometric triangles they are essentially inverted pyramids akin geometrically to the pyramids found around the globe that are intended to absorb knowledge and energy from beyond Earth. These vortexes, however, are anti-pyramids. Their purpose is the sustenance of Lucifer and the destruction of human souls.

These vortexes abound with original energy provided by the Heavenly Father's four brothers but swollen more so by the additional energy of their current angelic inhabitants. The energy from these vortexes extend deep into the Earth, whether they be on land or in the ocean. They can affect our weather, our mental state, can cause physical, mental, and even mechanical problems. Such power, when understood fully, is very frightening. No human being could ever survive in one.

The Bible recounts the judgmental impact of these vortexes. Recall the story of Lot. In the time of Abraham, the region around the salt sea tore itself apart when the inhabitants of the rich and populous cities at the south end of the sea refused to listen to Lot's warning. As punishment, they were then swept into a boiling vortex opened by the cracking of the earth's surface. These inverted pyramids can devour the souls of wayward humans.

The largest vortexes help feed Lucifer. He pulls energy from them when their dark angelic inhabitants depart in search of new ways to sustain Lucifer's life force. What he once did for the Heavenly Father, Lucifer now needs others to do for him. This inversion is not ironic; it is part of the Divine Plan.

The original hierarchy of the celestial realm called on the archangels to provide energy to Lucifer. Lucifer, in turn, would provide life-sustaining energy to the Heavenly Father. Instead, Lucifer first absconded with some of the energy given by the archangels until his greed led him to taking all of it. Energy from archangels has a special appeal to Lucifer because its unusual frequency is similar to what was returned to him from the Heavenly Father.

The ethology of this new world is a dark reflection of the celestial order. These "fallen angels," known to us as demons, were stimulated by the reddish blood-like energy that flowed from Lucifer when he fell to Earth. It attracted them in the same manner as Heaven's uncreated light. Consequently, their role on Earth mirrored their role in Heaven, but in a dark, severe, and radical manner: taking life-sustaining energy from human beings and giving it to Lucifer for his sustenance. These fallen angels believe they would eventually be called back to Heaven, but that will never happen.

As directed by the Divine Plan, Lucifer is only permitted to summon three demons at a time from these earthly vortexes to do his bidding. When this summoning occurs, the Great Father sends the same number of loyal angels from Heaven to Earth. Angels ordered to Earth must pass by the Heavenly Father. He has the authority to prevent their migration or to allow them to pass. Sometimes he orders them to remain with him. Although there must be the same number of good and bad angels on Earth at any given time, the Heavenly Father doesn't realize these seemingly docile angels are actually more powerful than the fallen angels, the demons.

The rebellion and departure of the four mighty archangels would prove to be a hidden blessing for humanity. It allowed Jesus to ascend to the primacy of archangels, providing nourishment to the Heavenly Father. Their departure prevented any potential conspiracy against Jesus by jealous archangels.

The Heavenly Father soon realized the profundity of these changes, despite pining for fallen Lucifer. Unselfish and loving, Jesus set about nourishing the Heavenly Father during his time of great need and would continue to do so after returning to Heaven following his completed mission on Earth.

Jesus was aided by the ever-knowing Marguerita, who channeled additional energy to Jesus to pass on to the Heavenly Father. So ready and intense was Jesus's acceptance of his new responsibility, the remaining angels in heaven acknowledged Jesus as the true Son of God. The Heavenly Father, realizing how profound were the changes that had wracked the celestial realm, bestowed upon Jesus a title that would have been most fitting and appropriate for the fallen Lucifer: God of Light.

This newly created domain of our Heaven served as the spiritual domain for Marguerita, who, without the knowledge of the Heavenly Father, rescued and embraced Michael once again. Michael and Marguerita had always been inseparable. She was the well-spring of his life force, as she was for so many others. Their energies served as a loving cocoon for each other. Unfortunately, the immense cataclysm that shook the celestial realm had taken a severe toll on Marguerita.

The relationship between the Heavenly Father and Marguerita was complex. Recall how the Heavenly Father was truly ignorant of The One or the Divine Plan. Upon becoming sentient, the Heavenly

Father assumed he was the only living entity within the celestial realm. He considered himself to be ruler of the universe. His ignorance of Marguerita was shocking. He did not know that Marguerita was in fact his own mother. What he saw instead was a weak, shriveled spirit; an ugly, strange, and worthless soul. He did not realize her deplorable condition was because she sacrificed so much of her own energy for his sustenance. He thought her expendable from heaven.

The realization that Lucifer had transformed into Satan, had been expelled from the celestial realm, and now had Earth as his personal kingdom ultimately aroused great anger in the Heavenly Father. As Lucifer would surely need subjects for his new kingdom, the Heavenly Father chose to send Marguerita among the first group of seeds to populate Lucifer's earthly kingdom. Neither the Heavenly Father nor Lucifer realized that with Marguerita came Michael.

The Heavenly Father sent Marguerita to Earth believing Lucifer would change her. Truth be told, he didn't really care what Lucifer did to Marguerita, even if it resulted in his putting her to "death" via a deep, eternal sleep. Most of all, the Heavenly Father could not understand why Michael, a loyal archangel, so doted on her, showering her with his own pure life-giving energy. This seemed a wasteful effort as Michael radiated beauty while Marguerita appeared emaciated, depleted, and exhausted.

As the sole keeper of the Divine Plan, Marguerita had never revealed her true self to any of the celestial dynasty. That is why the Heavenly Father had so little regard for her. If anything, he was suspect of this odd creature and came to fear ill-begotten intentions. For that reason, he covered her with a dark energy that would result in great pain and suffering during her myriad incarnations on Earth.

The strength and goodness of Marguerita, born of The One, has allowed her to endure all earthly trial and tribulation. Her loyalty to the Heavenly Father and the Divine Plan has allowed her to show the Heavenly Father great respect, admiration, and love every time her human soul has returned to Heaven for spiritual renewal. She acts as a model and example to all of us.

Unknown to all except The One, Him, and the Supreme Creator, Marguerita/Michael did not take all their energy with them when they were sent to Earth. They left a great deal of it, and perhaps even most of it, in Heaven for future use. For the time will come for completion of the Divine Plan, what we call Armageddon, when all evil will be destroyed.

The cataclysmic events that transpired within the celestial realm had the supreme benefit of ridding the heavens of evil. Lucifer brought all that is evil with him to Earth. As we are all too well aware, the struggle between good and evil that Lucifer triggered in the celestial realm remains alive and well on our planet.

So Marguerita by choice, and Michael by intrinsic connection, were among the first group of celestial spirits sent to Earth by the Heavenly Father to populate Lucifer's kingdom of Earth. Lucifer remained ignorant as to where Marguerita and Michael came from, nor did he recognize their devotion to each other. All were to be subject to him. Little did he realize the role Marguerita and Michael were to play in his newfound realm. The Heavenly Father may have ordered them into this earthly realm, but their true role was to counter the power of free will given to the seeds who would awaken in Lucifer's kingdom. The Golden Light had inspired the Heavenly Father to give souls free will in the hope that Lucifer could be redeemed and allowed to return to the celestial realm to be with him.

Lucifer isn't threatened by Michael, but he should be. As we will soon learn, Michael has become incarnate. Lucifer knows he lives somewhere on earth. Out of arrogance, though, Lucifer expects Michael to join him sooner or later. Lucifer seeks him out constantly and tries to tempt Michael into joining him the same way Lucifer tempted Jesus during his forty days in the desert. Michael has had many earthly incarnations but has never succumbed to Lucifer. In truth, Michael doesn't fear Lucifer because Michael is the seed of The One and Marguerita. As much as Lucifer believes he was "handmade" by the Heavenly Father, possessing the same power he enjoyed in the celestial realm, he will never be able to conquer Michael.

The dynamic of free will would come to identify and symbolize human life on Earth. In the Heavenly Father's original thinking, free will was a loving gift to Lucifer and the human seeds. He envisioned these newly sprouting seeds of life to be able to honor Lucifer as their

God, but to always come back to the Heavenly Father upon completion of their Earthy journey. Free will would be fueled by love. They could then return to Earth as new life and share with Lucifer some of the life-sustaining energy they had received from the Heavenly Father.

It is important to emphasize again and again: The Heavenly Father is truly "Our Father." He is the entity chosen by The One to care for us until the end of the world. Without the Heavenly Father, we would not exist. He is the spiritual being selected to serve as our "God" according to the Divine Plan.

Free will became, consequently, a source of hope for all humanity because it prevents Lucifer from ever being able to completely overcome the human race. Yet Lucifer is entirely dependent on humankind making the conscious free will choice to honor him as "God" in order for him to survive and renew.

Free will exists nowhere else in our universe, only on Earth.

The Heavenly Father always looked for ways to
make Earth a place of love and peace.

Credit: adventtr

THE FOURTH CHAPTER

Genesis Revisited

The Heavenly Father never sought discord among his progeny. Before and after the celestial cataclysm, he looked for ways to make Earth a place of love and peace, hoping that Lucifer would eventually return to him. Together with Mother Nature, the Heavenly Father filled the Earth with beautiful colors, a spectrum of glory reminding him of Lucifer. Greenery symbolizes his love for Lucifer and is identified universally as the color of the life force. The bluish tears of energy shed by distraught angel's form all the water on earth. Our oceans, seas, and waters remind the Heavenly Father of those who surround him in Heaven, even the absent Lucifer.

Earth served as a representation and manifestation of both Lucifer and the Heavenly Father. The Heavenly Father believed, despite all that had transpired, Lucifer could be a potential source of goodness for all life in his new kingdom. The profusion of loving energy given to him by the Great Father and his four sons could serve as a blueprint for Lucifer and his new world. After all, there was peace throughout his brother's kingdoms, a peace he wanted for Lucifer's world.

It did indeed take millions of years or longer for Earth to develop from its primordial origins. In the fullness of time, the Heavenly Father ordained that Lucifer's Earth should be given both angelic and human seeds of life. While this power flowed forth from the Heavenly Father, thinking it his own volition, its origins resided with Marguerita, the Great Father, and the host of celestial beings.

The Heavenly Father split the angelic energies in two so Lucifer would have ever more subjects. He had hoped his son would teach human beings right from wrong so that the conflict that wracked the celestial realm would not happen on Earth. Unknown to him, however, the Great Father covered these seeds with a spiritual energy taken from his four other sons.

All the souls who would ever exist on Earth were given by the Heavenly Father to Lucifer in twelve groups over many years. When these seeds/souls first entered earth, they loved only the Heavenly Father. They felt joy, peace, and a sense of wonder, even though their minds had not yet developed fully. Only with further development would they experience the pure power of love. In fact, they didn't even recognize Lucifer because he remained hidden from them - somber, dejected, bewildered, and residing within his own cocoon of energy.

The human souls were not sent immediately to Earth because the Great Father believed Lucifer needed time to think about what he had done and might change his ways.

Each of these twelve groups of souls destined to inhabit the Earth was different. None had the same abilities as any other group but were instead blessed in different manners and degrees. Those in the first group who had been closest to Marguerita and Michael received some of their pure energy from the Great Father, the Golden Light, and, ultimately, The One. They have been, and continue to be, the most gifted people among us. They have great abilities to assist others in every important aspect of life. And as has been said throughout history, greater gifts demand greater responsibility.

An important truth to remember is that even though Earth was given to Lucifer, its inhabitants belong to the Heavenly Father. It is only by the urging and temptation of Lucifer and his minions, combined with the exercise of free will, that souls can give their lives to Satan, aka the Devil, the Evil One, Tempter, Serpent, or any of the other appellations by which he has become known throughout the world.

According to the Divine Plan, the first group of souls was placed on Earth near Lucifer. When each of the other eleven groups arrived, they were transported to other earthly locations by a designated angel. Lucifer did not make himself known to any of them until all twelve groups had arrived on Earth. Lucifer was drawn to the first bag of human seeds or souls because he felt what appeared to be his own energy in it. He did not realize it was Michael's.

These first groups commenced a process of spiritual renewal established by the Heavenly Father. As each soul returned to Earth after being renewed spiritually by the Heavenly Father, it remained with its cohort of origin until each member had completed that same process. Then they were taken to other locations on Earth to learn important lessons about life. Some of these lessons include knowing more about the Heavenly Father, learning different forms of prayer and adoration, and being able to appreciate fully the beauty of Earth. In this manner, Earth was populated very slowly and with great care according to the Divine Plan.

From the beginning the intention was that every human being would be unique. Humans received all necessary life-sustaining energies directly from Earth itself. Human spirits did not need to "eat" to survive. They had everything they needed. Earth had been created as a place of beauty and peace. The cycle of coming and going from the realm of the Heavenly Father provided regeneration and rejuvenation. In short, humans had love, peace, and joy in abundance.

These first souls didn't realize that these lessons from the Great Father were preparation for the future struggles humans would have against the horrific power of evil, a power that would grow ever more intense and luring till the end of time.

Keep in mind, if the Great Father could have interceded directly with Lucifer to change him, he would have; but it wasn't time yet for Lucifer to know the Great Father even existed or that the Divine Plan would hold Lucifer accountable for all the evil he would propagate on Earth.

Lucifer did not pay attention to these first souls who had arrived on Earth. He ignored this vanguard contingent because he was angry at having been cast out from the celestial realm. His anger grew even worse when he tried to secretly follow those souls back to heaven when they sought spiritual renewal. He thought he could find a way to return "home" but was stopped always by Marguerita's impassable barrier of the Angels of the Most High. He considered the Heavenly Father to be a God; that is what he wanted to be as well.

Lucifer desired infiltration into Heaven expressly to destroy the Heavenly Father. Every time Lucifer thought his subterfuge was working and he was approaching the gates of Heaven, he would suddenly fall back to Earth. Like Sisyphus, the sinner condemned in Tartarus to an eternity of rolling a boulder uphill only to watch it roll back down again, Lucifer tried repeatedly to enter Heaven only to be rebuffed each time. This constant failure frightened him immensely and aroused in him great anger and frustration.

Frustrated by being foiled relentlessly, Lucifer devised his revenge. He decided he would do everything possible to prevent humans from entering Heaven for spiritual renewal. His option, goal, and *modus operandi* were to get humans to choose not to enter Heaven by virtue of their own free will. It did not take long for him to realize, however, the short-sightedness of this thinking. When he recognized how much pure energy he lost when these souls were never renewed, he changed his thinking. He salivated over humans who wallowed in sin and impiety but who also achieved spiritual renewal before returning to Earth, ripe again for Satanic temptation.

Lucifer did not awaken from his fall on an Earth devoid of inhabitants. Mother Nature had already created animals to dwell on it. She still had affection for Lucifer that motivated preparation for his kingdom. Mother Nature had suffered a severe loss of energy during her own forceful separation from Lucifer. The Great Father and Marguerita replenished this lost energy so Mother Nature could assist the Heavenly Father in creating Earth.

The animals created by Mother Nature were spiritual animals - not physical, corporeal animals. Their intrinsic energy was similar to the energy of the good angels who had been sent to Earth to establish balance with the fallen angels. Remember, these good angels were created by the Heavenly Father with energy unknowingly given to him by the Great Father.

The original inhabitants of Lucifer's kingdom (the angelic, human, and animal forms) were sparks of energy without defined figures. None possessed internal organs. They were transparent. While all human spirits looked the same, their uniqueness and individuality came from the particular energy imbued in them from the original human groupings.

In accordance with the Divine Plan, animals were placed on Earth primarily to be friends with humans. Specifically, animals were created to show humans how to love. Underscoring their close relationship with one another, the Great Father gave both animals and humans a special grace that enabled them to communicate with one another telepathically. They were able to share love through this telepathic communication. Love was all that was needed; there was no need for knowledge. Love begot happiness. They have a spiritual form that made them look physical though they were without corporeal expression.

The Divine Plan was that animals and humans were meant to live forever in peace. Humans were to learn from animals who, in fact, were more intelligent than humans at the beginning of life on Earth. Animals have a different soul and purpose than humans. One consequence is that animals do not need to return to the Heavenly Father to be renewed the way humans do.

When Lucifer first encountered animals, he asked them if they loved the Heavenly Father. If they replied in the affirmative, he would negate their existence by taking all their energy, rendering them inactive and essentially lifeless. So prevalent was the love for the Heavenly Father among animals, Lucifer became angry at them. Animals were also loving and caring toward humans but not toward Lucifer.

The only animal on Earth who chose loyalty to Lucifer was the snake. Yet even the snake did so more out of fear than true devotion. As a result, the snake, the serpent, became Lucifer's friend and eventually a symbol of evil.

As soon as the original group of twelve human and angelic seeds had been sent to Earth, Lucifer began stealing energy from them. It was then that Lucifer had his own epiphany. He decided the time had come for him to make known his presence as Earth's ruler.

To the surprise of all these spiritual creatures (human, angelic, and animal) there rose up an incredibly beautiful and powerful angel. Even though Lucifer had been on Earth the entire time, this was when every creature became aware of his presence and power. Almost immediately, he began to tempt them.

It is here that we must state forthrightly and profoundly the existence of life forms on other planets, in other cosmic kingdoms. Even before Earth was seeded with angels and humans, life forms from other worlds had visited Earth to examine the animal spirits. Lucifer, in his cunning and craftiness, convinced these spiritual visitors to draw life-sustaining energy from Earth's animals and to give it to him.

These spiritual visitors were subjects of the other four sons of the Great Father, the Heavenly Father's brothers. Some of their subjects had been sent to Earth to investigate what was happening and how they could be of assistance to the youngest of the five sons of the Great Father, namely, our Heavenly Father. Lucifer was impressed by the visitor's powerful energy. Try as he may, though, he never received any life-sustaining energy from them.

Instead, these visitors helped themselves to many human and animal creatures, taking them back to their home planets for investigation and experimentation. This occurred multiple times over eons. They also took back, unknowingly, a tiny amount of Lucifer's evil energy. It is this evil energy, acting like a foreign virus or mold, that will gradually spread and cause serious problems in each of those four kingdoms. A universal pandemic had begun.

Seeking to avoid the conflagration that had rent asunder the celestial realm, the Heavenly Father established rules, commandments, to teach human beings the proper way of living. Foremost among these was forbidding the taking of another person's life force, what we know now as killing. His antagonism toward the Heavenly Father in firm resolve, Lucifer commanded his angels to seek out and take life-sustaining energy from humans. More so, he encouraged humans to take life forces from animals by whatever means necessary.

To placate fear of usurping the Heavenly Father's commandments, Lucifer claimed to all that the Heavenly Father could neither see nor hear what they were doing. He urged them to just do whatever they themselves believed to be good. Consequently, some animals perished when humans took their life energy by force. This elicited a craving for the scent and color of blood. To Lucifer and his warped way of thinking, he saw this blood lust as a form of love, a trait we continue to see among humankind's most dastardly serial murderers. He convinced the souls that the shedding of blood would please the Heavenly Father.

There is not a location on Earth today where blood has not been shed. Blood has an energy that can influence us. It is like a mold that attracts more bloodshed. Blood excites Lucifer but can also weaken him.

Lucifer successfully altered the original intention of the Heavenly Father when populating the Earth with subjects for his deposed son. As humans embarked on a campaign of killing, avarice, and greed, the pure energy with which they had been created slowly but dramatically began to change in form.

Humans and animals began to develop corporeal forms even though neither was ever supposed to possess a physical body. By developing physical bodies, they were no longer inhabitants of a purely spiritual dimension on Earth. No longer could humankind, as spirit form, effortlessly glide above the ground. Instead, humans were compelled to walk on the Earth with animals.

The transition from spirit form to incarnate being resulted in significant changes in human and animal ontology. When solely spiritual beings, humans and animals were at risk of being drained of energy by fallen angels and demons. Once both took on corporeal form, animals and humans began to eat each other's flesh to obtain these same life forces. In killing one another, animals and humans gained greater power for self-protection but in so doing violated one of the cardinal rules set forth by the Heavenly Father.

When both humans and animals had evolved into physical forms, humans could no longer take spiritual energy from animals as they had in the past. They had to eat their flesh. Humans would have developed into a higher species if they had refrained from this particular transformation.

As sin grew and spread throughout Earth, the sanctity of life diminished to the point where animals and humans began to kill even their own kind. Humankind's thinking became so deranged that it came to believe eating the heart of a fellow human or animal was a sought-after delicacy possessing special powers. This unfortunate turn of events delighted Lucifer. It pronounced his dominance over the Earth. It did not, though, bring him any closer to his ultimate goal of ruling Heaven.

The power of Lucifer grew so strong he was able to influence humans to end their own life for various "good reasons." The more humans turned away from the Heavenly Father, the more Lucifer was able to engulf and convince them to misuse free will to end their lives. In a horrid reversal, the Heavenly Father's greatest creation, the human being, no longer knew or cared about what the Heavenly Father taught. Humankind alone began to determine what was right, good, and just for themselves. To put it bluntly, humans began to think of themselves as "gods."

Lucifer believed the shedding of blood, be it human or animal, would please the Heavenly Father. He was wrong. The mere sight of blood forced the Heavenly Father to slip into a state of repose as he heard the cries of each human being and animal killed on Earth. Lucifer has always taken delight in the shedding of blood. This plasma attraction extended to humans who have also developed a taste for blood and flesh.

This thinking became so perverse, humans began to think one could return to Heaven for renewal before one's designated time by killing another human and taking that person's place. Consequently, life became ever more violent and unbalanced. The triumph of human ego resulted in pervasive sadness and depression. There was no longer joy in life as there had been while being dutiful subjects of the Heavenly Father. Humans began to experience physical and spiritual hunger. Communication of any kind became difficult. The ultimate result was the growth of hatred. Evil became a form of excitement akin to a narcotic high.

Because of the many changes they had brought upon themselves, humans began to develop vocal cords. This facilitated communication in the physical dimension as telepathic capabilities diminished, but in a much less effective manner. Good news is that in the future, humans and animals will once again be able to communicate by interpreting the energy flowing first from their minds and then through their mouths. Language will no longer be a barrier to communication and understanding.

It is also true that humans can communicate with animals, if they so desire. And even though humans share many facial and other physical characteristics with animals, especially gorillas, apes, and monkeys, this relationship is not through evolution as many believe. It is, rather, through the act of divine creation.

As humans developed corporeal presence, they no longer remained in their designated planetary domains to learn life's important lessons. They went instead in search of animals, sought out their hiding places, and reveled in killing them, hoping this would provide the energy needed to survive.

Mother Nature became angry and distressed at the way human seeds were changing. They were becoming detrimental and harmful to her loving Earth. Reverence and respect for her creation dissipated. With deep concern she called out to both the Heavenly Father and Lucifer to do something about this horrifying turn of events. To her shock and utter surprise, neither answered her or even seemed to care. Lucifer had, after all, rejected her in the celestial realm, a rejection Mother Nature did not take lightly. The indifference of the Heavenly Father and Lucifer served to redouble her dedication to her planetary creation. If necessary, she was determined to renew Earth on her own.

To accomplish this daring undertaking, Mother Nature designed and implanted similar organs in both humans and animals. Each was given a heart, the beating of which was to replicate the energy of love flowing forth from the Heavenly Father. Other distinct physical features came from the Heavenly Father's four brothers. It is important to note, however, that humans and animals were separate and distinct creations; they were never intended to combine or unite physically.

Humans, in fact, shared greater blame for the increasing violence between the species. When humans realized the extent of their departure from the Heavenly Father's intention and the degree to which their actions caused such harm to Earth and its other inhabitants, they bent over like animals in an attempt to hide from the Heavenly Father. They even devolved to crawling as they couldn't bear to look at the Heavenly Father's countenance. After a long period of time, they began to walk erect again.

The many physical and metabolic resemblances between humans and animals exist because Mother Nature hoped such a degree of similarity would mitigate the urge to hurt and kill each other. If this could be imparted to them both, then perhaps peace might be restored to Earth, as intended from the very beginning into eternity.

With the help of his four sons, the Great Father also intervened in this effort with Mother Nature's knowledge. He gave the Heavenly Father the energy necessary to create a new organ for humans and animals: brains. The Heavenly Father then passed energy along to Lucifer for fulfillment of this intention. Lucifer could have kept this energy for his own use, but he chose not to because he believed human souls would never turn against him. Such was his arrogance, one of his greatest weaknesses.

The Great Father intervened because he wanted the Heavenly Father to know that Earth's occupants were beginning to show greater love and fidelity toward Lucifer than the Heavenly Father. To counter this degenerate shift in love and loyalty, he took energy from each of his four sons and funneled it to the Heavenly Father, who then passed it along to Lucifer. He hoped this brain adaptation, a physical nexus for the exercise of free will, would lead to a lessening of violence and killing by allowing each to distinguish between good and evil.

The conscience is a spiritual covering that attaches itself to humans at the moment of conception. It is part of the human seed and is the purview of the guardian angel. The role of the guardian angel is to lead us to making the right decision, oftentimes at odds with our free will. Sadly, despite having a conscience and the efforts of guardian angels, humans freely gave in to Lucifer's temptations.

Whenever a human spirit allowed itself to be tempted by Lucifer to take vital life forces from animals, this action caused the animal to weaken and, in some cases, die. In response to this serious alteration of the Divine Plan, Mother Nature began to create stronger and faster animals. From these arose dinosaurs, creatures who could withstand this assault from human spirits. Nevertheless, a survival of the fittest mentality began to take hold across the planet. Humans devised ways of dominating animals, then each other. This way of living is contrary to the Divine Plan and results in dire consequences, as we witness on a daily basis in our current world.

The Earth abounded then, and abounds still, with countless angelic presences. We are talking about numbers exceeding billions. Each angel has a designated purpose to accomplish. This role, and the amount of strength and energy required to accomplish it, is what distinguishes one angel from another. You could say that angel "DNA" lies in its explicit purpose. Its "chromosomes," however, are the unique expression of love from its maker. At the beginning of life on Earth, however, these angelic spirits could only watch and observe what was happening.

Angels share their energy with humans. This is why it is possible for humans to communicate with angels. Amazingly, very few humans partake of this capability.

Conversely, humans accelerated communication with Lucifer. They did this when they could no longer find happiness on their own and wondered whether following Lucifer could compensate for such existential angst. This allowed Lucifer to control and manipulate humans even more. In a show of insidious subterfuge, fallen angels absconded with energy from humans and funneled it to Lucifer. Lucifer, in turn, fed the egos of humans with this stolen energy. They rewarded him with ever greater reverence, thus making them ever more submissive to the Evil One.

While his kingdom filled with evil, Lucifer loved to taunt the Heavenly Father. Lucifer would call out to the heavens, "Look what your children are doing. They don't really love you. I don't want them. Why don't you take them back? They have no regard for human or animal life. They don't believe their life, all life, is a precious gift from you!"

Lucifer pleads for the gates of Heaven to be opened, but the Heavenly Father is no longer fooled. He knows Lucifer is responsible for what humans and animals have become. He also understands Lucifer needs to take energy from humans with the help of fallen angels to sustain his own life. Despite all this, however, the Heavenly Father still loves Lucifer, albeit to a lesser degree than before. He knows he must stop the spread of Lucifer's evil on Earth.

This evil grows more powerful each day humankind turns away from the Heavenly Father. Fortunately, the Divine Plan assures us that Lucifer will never achieve all that he desires. The bodies of humans may have changed but not their souls. The Great Father knew humans would not be able to remain in spirit form forever. The Great Father knows spiritual energy is much more powerful than physical energy, although physical energy is more attractive and appealing.

For years beyond knowing, the human race has continued to freely draw further and further away from the Heavenly Father. With three-fourths of the energy Lucifer extracted from the Heavenly Father, he now controls three-fourths of Earth. As a result, human beings no longer possess and exude the beautiful energy with which they were created. They no longer feel as alive as they once did. That is how deeply sin has detracted from their original splendor.

This attraction to Lucifer is based on false promises, assurances he can double the joy of whatever sin they are experiencing at present. It is no different than a drug dealer supplying an ever more lethal dose of narcotics. When a human being gives its life force to Lucifer, it is a form of worshipping him. Humanity gave its love to him willingly, infected as it were by the virus of sin. That is why sin is now pandemic.

Through the proliferation of sin and corruption of its life force, the human soul no longer radiates its original pure pristine energy. Negative, polluted, destructive energy now prevails. This encompassing negativity is even affecting demons. They are becoming weaker, unable to provide Lucifer the volume of human source nutrients he needs for survival. Consequently, Lucifer is growing weaker, but our joy must be tempered, he remains a tremendously powerful foe.

Lucifer continues to corrupt humanity with energy soiled by his hatred toward the Heavenly Father. He experiences no greater joy than when this same poison infects human souls. It is an unfortunate fact of life that every one of us is affected to some degree by the power of evil. That is why Earth will eventually be destroyed because of our turning away from the Heavenly Father.

At one time, Lucifer was the most beautiful and powerful archangel. His wayward journey into hate and deceit has robbed him of this majesty. Like a faded Hollywood star, though, he will do anything to try to maintain that faded, long-gone beauty. It isn't working. The more he applies "makeup and plastic surgery," the greater the realization of his faded glory. Even fellow demons are wondering what is happening to their "God" and why.

Ironically, it can be said that desperation is the father of brilliance. Lucifer, therefore, is redoubling efforts at spreading hatred all over the world. The greatest manifestation of societal hatred is war. And the fuel for this destructive energy comes mostly from the killing of innocents.

Lucifer is presently calling more and more angels out of their Earth vortexes to carry out his plan for spiritual warfare. He believes they can somehow obtain the energy he needs. The fallen angels are his army legions. All the traditional ways of spreading evil are still used by him, even as he seeks to develop new ones. It is akin to Hitler's dreams of "super weapons" turning the tide of World War II.

Time is of the essence for him and us. Fortunately, when fallen angels depart their Earth vortexes to attack humanity, good angels are there to stare them down. They do this by showing the fallen angels what they will become at the day of judgment and what will eventually happen to them. Their greatest weapon in this standoff is showing what Lucifer looked like in his glory and what he looks like now.

Lucifer pleads still to the Heavenly Father, arguing that Heaven should be his kingdom. Not surprisingly, he also mocks the Heavenly Father. He is the ultimate bipolar being. Hell doesn't exist yet, but one can see a preview of it in his eyes. The love infused in him at his creation as a gift to the Heavenly Father is long gone. Stated simply and directly: hell is a state of being where there is no love.

Lucifer enjoys showing the Heavenly Father how much death and destruction human beings have caused, how their souls have become infused with evil. He will never admit his culpability for humanity's sins, even though human beings frequently kill through his urging and motivation. He has worked endlessly with fallen angels to darken human souls by taking the creative energies of light, truth, beauty, and love from their souls. Evil has become more important to humanity than good, and we do not even realize it.

No matter how much blood is shed, it is never enough for Lucifer. Human greed developed as a consequence of his unending desire for blood. Only love can cleanse and renew us. Love is our solitary hope. That is why prayers and blessings are very important sources of divine energy. They are gifts from the Heavenly Father. A golden energy goes out from wherever people gather to pray. Our prayers help to cap the vortexes of the fallen angels. It is imperative for humanity to turn away from Lucifer's temptations and back to the love of the Heavenly Father. Lucifer has no love to offer. He is incapable of loving.

Lucifer wants the Heavenly Father to cut this cord of life to each of us. He doesn't want us to be able to return to the Heavenly Father renewed with his love, returning to Earth with the desire to live a better incarnation because of what we have felt and learned during our process of spiritual revitalization.

Lucifer has had every opportunity to transform his being because of his mother, Marguerita. He doesn't desire or want her love, only her pure energy. He hopes he can use this additional power to enter Heaven again and take over the role of the Heavenly Father. He wants to rule both Heaven and Earth. It will never happen. The power of Marguerita comes directly from The One and is much greater than what he, or we, can imagine.

Lucifer is so powerful. He is, in fact, larger than Earth. He is not on Earth. He surrounds Earth. It functions as his playground and toy. If nothing else, that should convince us how much we need the Heavenly Father.

To counter the malignancy that is Lucifer and his minions, the Great Father is creating more angels. Some are being given to the

Heavenly Father to sustain and protect him. Others are being sent to Earth to counter the great number of demons Lucifer has summoned from the vortexes. These demons are more powerful than many of the earlier ones because they have been resting longer and therefore growing stronger. They have also learned how to pull energy from many places on Earth, especially those where hatred has festered and ruled for countless centuries.

There is, however, dissension among the demonic ranks. Some demons do not want to leave their vortexes when Lucifer calls them. They are comfortable there and would like to remain ensconced within these volcanic catacombs. Lucifer, though, needs the strength they alone can obtain for him.

When demons do come out, they do it in groups of three. There is a sense in which Lucifer is jealous of them because they don't depend on him for their life forces. They need not call out continually seeking nourishment from the Heavenly Father.

The good angels being sent to Earth now are stronger than these native evil demons, but they will not obtain full maturity until they have received additional energy and life forces from the Great Father. That energy is to be received over a long period of time and in small doses. It should be noted that the angels charged with holding our crumbling Earth together are constantly being given the energy they need.

Throughout all that happened in Heaven and Earth, Marguerita's heart was heavy with sorrow. This is entirely understandable as she was the mother not only of the Heavenly Father, but of Lucifer too. Her love for Lucifer was strong. Still, she could not condone in any way his disobedience in turning away from the Heavenly Father.

The Heavenly Father, in turn, was not aware of her feelings at the time. By the time he did become cognizant of Marguerita's disappointment, he had already firmly established Lucifer's reign on Earth and could not change his free will decision. Lucifer will never forget her because she is the mirror through which he sees himself, especially the evil he was doing. He will always love to hate her.

Just as human beings have guardian angels as their conscience, Lucifer has Marguerita. He loved her from afar in Heaven, but he hates her on Earth because she wants him to realize he is nowhere near as omnipotent as he thinks and will be held responsible for what he has done. From a purely human perspective, we wouldn't want to live any longer if we knew only the presence and impact of evil and not the power of good. Life is not life without hope.

If the Heavenly Father had not given so much power to Lucifer, enabling his transformation into what he was never intended to be, Marguerita would have joined Lucifer out of maternal love. Lucifer was her rebellious son, but he never pushed her aside in Heaven the way he had Mother Nature. His motivation remains the pursuit of power to overthrow the Heavenly Father, and he sees Marguerita as a potential ally. Make no mistake, though, Lucifer will never become a prodigal son.

Marguerita's role on Earth has been to stop the Heavenly Father from showering Lucifer with love. In every earthly incarnation, she has worked for a world peace that would allow us to grow closer to the Heavenly Father, helping us recognize and cherish just how special we are to him. She will continue to be a source of wisdom and love for all life on Earth.

To fight evil, one must know how evil works and why it exists. Such is the purpose of this revelation. Reuniting Heaven and Earth is the ultimate objective. While Marguerita makes sure Lucifer never rests, Jacobin's role is preventing Lucifer from drawing energy from souls on Earth. Granted, at times it seems Jacobin is losing the battle, but the Divine Plan guarantees the ultimate triumph of good over evil. To that end, Jacobin must become the being he was created to be: Michael the Archangel. Michael stands as the source of justice and strength that will finally, and decisively, allow good to prevail over evil at the end of the world.

Lucifer is now only a shell of what he was once. He is filled with many crags and holes. His light is much dimmer, though he can still project himself for very short periods of time, an apparition of his former self. It is enough to fool his followers. This is the direct result of the Heavenly Father cutting off the already meager flow of energy to Lucifer. It is the awakening of clear sight. Previously, the Heavenly Father did not want to see the evil spreading over the Earth. Now he wants and needs to see it. We are children of the Heavenly Father. We belong to him and not Lucifer. The Heavenly Father loves us. Lucifer hates us.

Angels from the Great Father are presently dissolving the layer of negative energy Lucifer had placed successfully around the Heavenly Father to control him. As that energy falls over Earth and dissipates, the fallen angels are wondering what is happening. They feel the change. Some of them are even beginning to see the evil Lucifer has caused.

This may have started the countdown to Armageddon. Fallen angels turning away from Lucifer before the end of time is antecedent to their being sent to one of many different levels of existence. They will not be able to share Heaven with those who have been judged as good and faithful servants, but in a small way their self-punishment will be mitigated by a showing of love.

The power of love was experienced each time a human
soul was renewed by our Heavenly Father.

Credit: VladGans

The Cycle of Life Explained

As its very beginning, Earth was a spiritual kingdom at peace. Human life in its spiritual form experienced nothing but joy. Nothing physical existed. All forms of life communicated with one another either telepathically or through some form of shared energy: God, angel, humans, animals, and nature. Life was created to remain that way forever. The first sin - deviation from the will of the Heavenly Father - had not yet occurred.

The power/energy of love was experienced each time a human soul was renewed spiritually by the Heavenly Father. His love nourished and sustained everyone and everything. Love perpetuated, sustained, and gave purpose to one's sentience. Each time a soul returned to the Heavenly Father, this love increased within you and sparked ever greater joy.

A soul had no desire for greater love. There was no need to eat or drink or for any kind of corporeal nourishment. Time did not exist. The beauty of Earth gave comfort. The Earth was far more beautiful than anything we see today. Its spectrum of colors was more vivid, much brighter, and blanketed the Earth with creative energy.

Stated simply and forthrightly: it was truly Heaven replicated on Earth, prior to the cataclysm that would rock the celestial realm and before the evil Lucifer would unleash in his planetary kingdom.

The structure of Earth had some weaknesses, but love filled all forms of life on it.

Life was everlasting, as it remains today, but without concepts of time or eternity. One was simply cognizant of self. There was individual awareness. Even when the energy of your spiritual being was in the process of renewal, you never lost your sense of identity. There was no sin, no death, and no need for judgment. Heaven and Earth alone existed. There was no hell.

The source of all life is its unique soul. It is the energy, the life force of love with which we were created by the Heavenly Father, souls bestowed to Lucifer for our care on Earth. Every human seed has lived at least once on Earth. Angels have been on Earth since they were first joined to Lucifer in the original dispersal of human seeds. All the energy with which the Heavenly Father created the myriad forms of life remains connected to him until the end of time.

As their intellects expanded, humans began to understand that life is an unending process. According to the type and amount of energy with which a human soul has been endowed, the length of its life on Earth was already determined. What remains unknown is the number of earthly lives that soul will experience. Humans are required to choose how long one wants to spend in any particular life within the full amount of time given to you.

Returning to the Heavenly Father for renewal was an essential part of being. When that time arrived, arms were extended upwards toward Heaven. This was an indication the soul was ready to be renewed spiritually. At that instant, the soul's guardian angel and the archangel of death carried the human spirit to Heaven. The guardian angel would receive a special gift for having helped care for that soul.

It was only after human consciousness deepened that humans became aware of being taken to the Heavenly Father. All they knew previously was that this process was an exchange and replenishment of love. The result was overwhelming feelings of ever more abundant peace and joy. This cycle of replenishment continued throughout each life, however long it lasted.

When the guardian angel brought the renewed soul back to Earth, it was joined to others in the group with whom it had originally entered Earth. Oftentimes, these groupings were taken to other worldly locations to learn important truths and lessons. This spiritual renewal served not only to increase love within that soul, but also to help, sustain, and improve other lives. Life was all about loving, not just knowing. This cycle of renewal is constant throughout the celestial hierarchy, save for The One who is loving, all-good, just, and eternal.

It is fact that life was designed to be perfect. It took the gift of 'free will" for sin and destructive energies to take hold throughout the Earth. That is when everything began to change. The development of a physical dimension to human existence replaced the creative powers of love with its antithesis: destructive impetuses imperiling love and life itself. These destructive, often uncontrollable forces gave birth to hatred. Hatred is the imitation and reflection of Lucifer's rebellious comportment.

As human beings chose to freely turn away from the Heavenly Father's love toward behaviors forbidden by him (for example, killing animals and one another), the very nature of humankind began to change. Spiritual beings developed physicality, morphing away from their spiritual origin in proportion to their rejection of the Heavenly Father and acceptance of Lucifer's direction.

The timing of spiritual renewal, our willful return to the Heavenly Father, suffered an unfortunate reversal: it became an occasion of fear rather than a desired reunion. What had initially been welcomed as an opportunity for spiritual renewal became distorted by the emergence of sin, death, pain, and suffering on Earth. Death is Lucifer's curse. This was the most unfortunate result of sin. It is what Lucifer wanted, because viewing the time for spiritual renewal (i.e., death) as a denial of life blinded humankind to just how precious, powerful, and important is the renewal of spiritual energy, namely, the love of the Heavenly Father.

This fear of spiritual renewal exists still. That is why some humans refuse entry into Heaven. There is a futility in this refusal because all souls must be judged eventually, not just by the Heavenly Father but by oneself reflecting on the recently passed incarnation. Final judgment on each individual soul, its many lives on Earth, will occur at the end of time. That is when the Heavenly Father will guide us as we judge the sum total of our soul's free will choices made over multiple incarnations on Earth.

The way in which humans viewed life changed dramatically. This drastic alteration of the Divine Plan turned life into a struggle for physical survival more than spiritual revival. The spiritual aspect of existence became increasingly ignored, neglected, and, for many, lost. Consequently, the process of spiritual renewal changed as well. New ways had to be found to sustain humankind's spirit. Sin destroyed much of the spiritual dynamic within the human soul. It so covers the soul with destructive energy that people can no longer tell the difference between good and evil. Shocking still: many do not even want to know the difference.

This is only part of Lucifer's capabilities with regards to Earth domination. His power of temptation is pervasive and ubiquitous. He wants to repeat on Earth what he did in Heaven. There, he stole three-fourths of the life-sustaining energy he was supposed to funnel to the Heavenly Father. He seeks to steal as much, if not more, from his human subjects. As it was his disobedience and defiance that instigated the celestial turmoil, he seeks this same disobedience and defiance among humankind toward the Heavenly Father.

This attitude among humankind was intended to show the Heavenly Father that human beings loved Lucifer more. He believed the Heavenly Father would be weakened significantly from not receiving the energy of love humans were to have brought him. This kind of thinking betrayed his Achilles' heel. For when human beings chose not to be renewed and failed to receive the gift of the Heavenly Father's pure energy of love, Lucifer had little to steal from them for himself, the very energy he craved and needs for his well-being.

Lucifer's conniving is motivated by his unending desire to return to Heaven and overpower the Heavenly Father. It is an exercise in futility. It can never happen. It is akin to picking a piece of fruit from a tree: you can never put it back.

Lucifer's scheming succeeded in impressing the fallen angels as to his power and prominence. They remembered what he had promised them in Heaven. As a result, they gladly embarked on draining life-sustaining energy from human beings and giving it gladly to Lucifer. This insidious exploit not only sustained Lucifer, but it stopped human beings from overcoming the effects of sin in the world by using the renewed energy they would have received from the Heavenly Father.

Lucifer is much more powerful than he is intelligent. The very purpose of his creation was to provide life-sustaining energy to the Heavenly Father. This responsibility did not require much in the way of intelligence. The inherent danger in this arrangement is that such power is often exercised without much thought and can easily become self-defeating. Lucifer's mind-set is basically adolescent. He actually thought his display of power would make the Heavenly Father proud of him and welcome him back to Heaven as a repentant son. It made him, instead, a pathetic figure.

Like lava flowing from a volcano, evil spread rapidly over the Earth through the destructive power of sin. Though Lucifer was the source of this negativity, it did not possess the energy and power needed to sustain him. Only good energy, especially pure energy, can do that. As a result, he is no longer the great spiritual being he used to be. Do not be fooled, however. He is still frightfully powerful.

Lucifer cannot stop the process of spiritual renewal. It is necessary and exists, but it is not nearly as effective as it was in the past because life has been harmed deeply by the power of sin. The myriad effects of sin cannot be removed completely. Traces remain in souls even after being renewed spiritually by the Heavenly Father. That is why it is absolutely essential to supplement the process of spiritual renewal while souls are still on Earth. Such is the importance of the sacrament of reconciliation offered by the Church.

Urgency springs from the fact that many today do not believe death is necessary in order to be spiritually and physically reborn through reception of love directly from the Heavenly Father. There is still an appointed time in life when we are scheduled to return to the Heavenly Father. That timing, though, is largely determined by us when we chose a way of life we believe will make us better. One's appointed time may, however, be shortened by another person's hatred and homicidal actions. When such tragic events occur, the time lost in that lifetime must be added to another of that soul's incarnations.

When the moment to return to Heaven comes, our spirit separates from our body which had acted like a shell over it. When spirit separates from body, the body cannot sustain itself. It dies. This is the beginning of the process called death. It is, though, only the end of this particular earthly incarnation. Life never ends. We return again and again in a continual spiritual/physical regeneration.

A human being possesses only one soul, and this spirit must be renewed as earnestly as possible. Souls reenter Earth through the process of procreation. A new physical body is provided for the returning soul, but it is the same soul, implanted in a new body and with another important lesson to be learned during the commencing lifetime. Even though we inhabit a new body, we retain the unique energy composition that has made us unique for all eternity. It is basically our unique energy "fingerprint." No two souls are alike.

It is no surprise the Roman Catholic Church as many others do not believe in the concept of reincarnation. As understood by many, reincarnation denies many of the essential truths of the Church. The stumbling block has been the inability to reconcile spiritual renewal and reincarnation.

When the soul returns to Earth from its spiritual renewal in Heaven, it may still carry with it some of the effects of its past sins. These weaknesses can be reawakened by Lucifer's evil influence. The process of spiritual renewal is unfortunately not guaranteed; many have strayed from the process established by the Heavenly Father in love for his precious life seeds.

Lucifer believes life on Earth is nothing short of a curse. If he ever feels "happiness," it is only when humans use free will to believe in him and do his bidding, when they have willingly given their souls to him. The widespread evil on Earth is not the fault of any weakness of the Heavenly Father. It is entirely from human beings using their free will to give their lives, and therefore their energies, to the God of Darkness.

The original pure energy of the Heavenly Father that strengthened and cleansed the human soul in Heaven has diminished in the face of widespread evil on Earth. One's sins can be forgiven on Earth, but that human being must have firm resolve to overcome its chosen inclination toward evil. The good news is that the Heavenly Father's power of love and forgiveness still exists. It is offered to humanity always and without stipulation.

The journey of a soul after earthly death begins similarly for everyone. As soon as your last breath is taken, at its determined time, your guardian angel comes to your right side and your archangel of death appears on your left. With their hands under your shoulders, they carry you upward from Earth. You are told you should not be afraid because while this event in your life is called death on Earth, it is only yet another step on the path to final judgment in Heaven.

While still somewhat confused by what is happening, one's attention is drawn to incredible natural beauty, the perfection of all earthly imagery. This is augmented and enhanced by inspiring music emanating from all that you see. Most souls find it difficult to believe they have died and are transitioning into a different phase of being. It is natural to struggle against death as the human mind is pulled in many directions during this existential alteration.

The transitional soul is clothed in a spirit-like covering. The soul is taken first to what appears to be a shimmering blue river, only to learn it is a source of sacred energy. On the other side, you recognize people who have loved you and gone before. You no longer remember their names, but you are certain of their having loved you. You realize they are there to welcome you back. No words are spoken. Some of them may have already returned to Earth, but a portion of their total energy remains in Heaven.

The archangel of death asks if you would like to pass over to the other side. The lure and beckoning are strong, for in addition to the souls of loved ones gone before, there is the brilliant light emanating from the Heavenly Father. At this juncture you still have free will. It is up to the individual soul to decide the next step. While some souls may choose to enter the Light, they may first want to return to Earth. Such a decision can be made for many reasons. The newly deceased may miss loved ones. There may be responsibilities in need of completion or fulfillment.

A defined group of angels may permit this return to happen, but only if there is reason to believe the soul will undergo transformation by such a return. This occurs as a three-step process. In the first stage, the soul visits loved ones for whom there is genuine concern about mental health and physical well-being. In the second stage, there occurs the realization and relief that these loved ones are being cared for by their guardian angels. The third stage is the conclusive one: when the soul acknowledges and accepts it is time to go to the Light.

Many of those who opt not to go to the Light have a strong inclination toward evil. It could be because of how the most recent life on Earth was lived. For instance, that soul may be fearful of facing the Almighty's judgment. Lucifer's lure is so strong that the soul may want to continue its evil ways. Should that soul choose to return to Earth without completing the process of spiritual renewal, it can only do so as spirit, not in a physical body.

A soul who has made that choice is allocated a set amount of time to remain on the Earth. They are also only allowed to return three times. Once that limit is reached, that soul must go into a deep period of hibernation, reviving only during the Last Judgment, when it is time to review the sum total of lives lived, lessons learned, and unmet aspirations.

Still others choose to neither return to Earth nor advance into Heaven despite having a greater period of lives remaining. These confused souls reside in a state of limbo. It has not yet been revealed what will happen to them. It is one of the many mysteries remaining about our spiritual existence.

Those choosing to cross the "river" do so with the two angels who have served as transitional guides. Their final act is to transfer some of their angelic energy into the newly arrived soul. Once on the other side, the soul feels cared for and loved beyond description but this still is only the beginning of one's entry into Heaven.

Once the soul has reached the other side, its guardian angel departs and goes to a place where it can rest. Its departure ushers forth a brilliant cloud appearing before the soul. Behind it is a beautiful golden gate extending as far as the spiritual eye can see. From within the gates comes peaceful and comforting sounds generated by what looks like the wings of angels. The soul has finally entered Heaven.

Those souls who opt to return to Earth unfortunately cannot bring that euphoria back with them. They do not receive that angelic energy. This awareness coincides with multitude reports from people with near-death experiences who felt tremendous love during their brief sojourn in Heaven, only to express regret and remorse at having to return to Earth.

The soul who has entered Heaven is filled with warmth, comfort, and excitement. One's spiritual "body" floats in this ethereal atmosphere as angelic voices beckon it to come closer. They sing the most beautiful music ever heard. It is musical love and adoration, totally enveloping the soul.

The archangel of death departs. You enter a place of reflection and remain there in solitude. Here you examine only the last life lived on Earth. You experience the good that you did, as well as the bad, what you should have done, didn't do, and what you had hoped but failed to accomplish. Although the music is still beautiful, it slowly begins to change. The soul now experiences both joy and sadness from it, but not with the emotional affect a human being would feel while in a physical body.

All the reflected memories the soul reviewed from this past life are then collected. Two different angels come forward. Each holds what appears to be a brilliant golden container resembling a scale. They weigh the good and bad from this most recent earthly incarnation. While this is happening, the soul moves forward to yet another location in Heaven where further reflection is done on what it has seen and learned so far.

It is there the angels combine the good and bad collections into one. This allows the individual soul to decide by itself whether it has successfully lived the life aspired to the last time it came to Heaven for spiritual renewal and judgment. This detailed comparison provides solid comprehension of where you did good and where you fell short, by virtue of the effect your actions had on others and yourself.

Following this intense judgmental exercise and life critique, the soul falls into a very deep and restful sleep. It is like the sleep of death, the duration of which varies for each individual soul. When finally awakened, the soul is filled with great love. An archangel then reveals how much time that soul still has to return and experience life on Earth, asking what that soul has learned during this entire process.

At this juncture, the soul ponders and decides what it is it will seek to accomplish in the next life, if indeed another incarnation is available. No one helps the soul make that decision. It is the product of free will. What that soul has done in the recently concluded life greatly influences the choices made for the next embodiment.

Once this decision is made, the soul again rests. Just prior to leaving Heaven, the soon-to-be-incarnated soul is bathed by the light of the Heavenly Father, a parting blessing, but also a harbinger of the welcome that awaits you again after one finishes this new incarnation. We can call this the life line because it attaches us always to the Heavenly Father. Sometime thereafter, its new life - and purpose - on Earth begins.

Jesus's love is greater than any gift we could receive.

Credit: titoOnz

Jesus Becomes the Light of the World

Lucifer's descent to Earth came with an important caveat: he was given a specific amount of time by the Great Father to forego his egomaniacal ways, his avarice, his greed, and his desire for supremacy and dominance over the Heavenly Father. As we have seen, Lucifer emphatically declined to change. If anything, he redoubled his lust for power and dominance. He did not realize then, and has only realized of late, that he has lost favor with the Great Father for not following the rules of the universe.

After humans had devolved into physical form, the Heavenly Father sought ways in which to turn people away from the rapid increase of evil desired by Lucifer. The Heavenly Father knew something had to be done to improve the human condition on Earth. His foremost desire remained bringing Lucifer back to Heaven. In this way he could attest to all humanity the genuine love Lucifer possessed for the Heavenly Father. This is not, however, part of the Divine Plan.

Consequently, Lucifer's intransigence triggered the beginning of the end times. The ultimate struggle between good and evil had now begun and would be engaged by all the powers of Heaven. The One knew all that was going to happen. He had developed the Divine Plan to guide creation to its preordained and proper conclusion. This plan is inviolable, sacrosanct, will succeed, and be in effect until the end of time - without change.

Lucifer's actions on Earth deeply troubled the Heavenly Father. It wasn't what he had wanted or expected. The resulting confusion and concern drained much of his energy and forced him to rest for longer and longer periods of time. This debilitated condition made it ever more difficult for the archangel (who would come to be known on Earth as Jesus) to provide the Heavenly Father with the ever increasingly amount of life-supporting energy he needed.

Recall the male/female duality of all creation. Such was the nature of the archangel Jesus/Mary up until the time Jesus was elevated to feed the Heavenly Father. At that time Mary was separated from Jesus. She lapsed into a period of rest while Jesus assumed his new responsibility. Despite this separation, they remained interdependent. She also provided energy to the Heavenly Father through Jesus. The unity of these two made the decision to have Mary be the future mother of Jesus all the more coherent. That is why it wasn't a surprise in Heaven at all when this story unfolded on Earth.

The truth is that Jesus and Mary were selected for this role long before human seeds were created. They were even given a special energy of divine love to accomplish what they were being sent to do. That is also why Jesus and Mary had an unbreakable cord of life and wisdom connecting them to the Heavenly Father. The Heavenly Father, in turn, nourished Jesus and Mary with additional energy funneled to him by the Great Father.

The Heavenly Father did not realize the Divine Plan would be for Jesus to claim Earth as his own. He still hoped for conversion and reconciliation with Lucifer. This would never occur. The end result would be eternal acrimony between Jesus and Lucifer, a reprise of Lucifer and Jacobin's fratricide, a clash of good versus evil persisting until the end of human time.

The Heavenly Father's decision to order his most loyal Archangel to descend to Earth as a familial duo of salvation was actually part of the Divine Plan formulated by The One. In so doing, the Heavenly

Father chose to rely on the remaining ranks of archangels to assume greater responsibility in providing him with life-sustaining energy. Jesus would forego the aforementioned responsibility to undertake the soul-saving mission entrusted to him by the Heavenly Father. Lucifer could never become human because he had taken so much energy from the Heavenly Father that he had to remain the Archangel he was created to be.

Thus began the great miraculous adventure that would save humankind.

A very old, childless, and presumably barren woman by the name of Anna was chosen to be the mother of Mary. The Heavenly Father did so to demonstrate at once his incredible power to humankind, that he who created the physical and metabolic laws on Earth had the power to contravene them at will.

This awesome intervention would be witnessed by everyone in Anna's village when a sudden, mysterious ball of fire delivered both the seed of Mary and the seed of Jesus into the womb of Anna. People in the village were awestruck and frightened by this mysterious fireball. They could not see it impregnate Anna. As suddenly as it appeared, it seemingly vanished. No damage was caused nor was anyone hurt. The villagers quickly forgot about this mysterious incident from above. Anna and her husband Joachim, however, knew this child would be very special. This intuition would be verified further by other events surrounding and accompanying Mary's birth.

Mary was a simple, gentle child. Her early life was very quiet and uneventful. Without realizing it fully, though, she was being prepared for what the Heavenly Father would soon call on her to do. When she was a little older, an angel appeared to her in a dream. It inspired her to fast and pray for three days in the temple. While contemplating there, an old woman told her she would have a special role to play in the world. She asked Mary if she would be willing to give birth to a child no one else could bring into the world. We can only imagine the bewilderment and consternation this brought to the young girl's mind.

Not long after that temple visit, Mary had another dream in which a very bright light turned into a rainbow of brilliant colors.

She was visited by an archangel who told her that he was going to ask her a question and one time only. Before asking it, he showed her what the rest of her life would be like with Jesus, how he would suffer and die on a Roman cross. The archangel showed Mary the great anguish and heart-wrenching pain she would have to endure. The archangel explained that she would be the Mother of Heaven and Earth and concluded by asking if she would be willing to accept all he had shown her. Without fully understanding why, Mary replied, "Yes. If it is the will of God, I will give my heart and soul." She then fell into a profound sleep. When she awoke she did not remember what she had been shown and promised. It would, however, remain with her in the deepest regions of her subconscious.

Not long after this event, Mary discovered she was pregnant from the seed she had carried within her from Heaven. A widower named Joseph, a carpenter who had been an acquaintance of her father (Anna's husband), came to visit her. He told her about a dream he had two nights in a row. He explained how he was told Mary was pregnant and that he should marry her. Joseph was very embarrassed in recounting these dreams, because he was as old as her father had been before his death. With deep emotion and great concern, Joseph expressed fear she might, according to Jewish law, be stoned if found to be an unmarried woman with child.

They agreed, therefore, to be married as quickly as possible. Once this was accomplished, Mary moved into Joseph's home where some of his children still resided. They liked Mary; but were jealous of the love, affection, and concern Joseph showed toward Mary. Some of them were actually older than Mary and had children of their own. They could not understand why their father would marry her at his advanced age. They even doubted he was the father of the child. The women at the town well spread disparaging gossip about how strange it was for two people so different in age to be married.

Mary was a good wife and caring grandmother to Joseph's grandchildren. She and Joseph truly did love one another. It need be said, though, they never had sexual relations. Joseph had fulfilled what God had asked of him.

When Jesus was born, Mary thought, *My blood is upon him now, and his blood will be upon the Earth.* She pondered throughout her life as to why these words came to her then. Truth be told, Mary was very caring and loving, but she was not very intelligent in her earthly incarnation. She no longer thought about the angelic messages that had occurred in her dreams, nor did she possess on Earth any of the knowledge that she was an archangel of the Heavenly Father.

This ignorance was a blessing. It protected her and Jesus from Lucifer. For Lucifer stood on guard as he feared time and circumstance might be ripe for divine intervention into his earthly kingdom. He feared the arrival of a child who might grow to become a threat. To counter this, he motivated King Herod, a demented ruler who enjoyed the sight of blood as much as Lucifer did, to do his bidding.

For all his demonic power, Lucifer is a curious and fragile creature. He possesses limited intelligence compensated by a voracious ego. Perhaps the best historical reference would be Adolf Hitler. Engorged with early triumph, Hitler failed ultimately because of his ego and unwillingness to listen to anything other than his own demented inner voice. Lucifer, likewise, can only keep so much in his mind at one time. He is not omniscient.

Human minds function differently than the minds of angels or other supernatural beings. The human mind possesses four levels. No one gets to the second level without divine intervention. Mary and Jesus were extremely special, but their minds came off as like any other human being entering Lucifer's kingdom on Earth.

Little demons called "watchers" record for Lucifer what every soul says and does on earth. These "watchers" were among the last cohort of angels created by the Great Father. To this band of Satanic spies, Jesus seemed slightly strange but no more so than other humans inhabiting Earth. These other strange minds helped to shield and protect Mary and Jesus. This allowed their early years together to be quiet and uneventful, perfect for preparing to do the will of the Heavenly Father.

Jesus received increasing public attention as a young boy teaching in the temple. He instructed religious scholars, answered their questions, held forth with the most learned among them - all without realizing the source of this wisdom or why he was doing it.

An old woman in the temple had begun to teach and reveal many things to him. These were things he often did not want to hear, yet alone believe. Mary did not like this old woman, but she allowed her to instruct Jesus because it seemed the right thing to do. Mary learned to trust her intuition, guided as it was by the Holy Spirit. This was the same old woman who had spoken to Mary on previous occasions and had served Mary as midwife during Jesus birth in the manger.

Jesus remained within his village during his adolescence. Both he and his mother Mary continued, without realizing it, to prepare for what was about to happen. It was a combined sense of anticipation and foreboding. Mary would tell Jesus about the miracle of his birth, but he respectfully did not believe her.

When Jesus started his public ministry years later and his teaching became regionally acclaimed, he became a threat to those same religious leaders he had met as a young boy in the temple. The evil power of Lucifer had already begun to influence and dwell in them. Demons recognized and glared at Jesus's exceptionality. They were furious he was able to expel them by his own authority; no other exorcist possessed that kind of power. In so doing, Lucifer became aware of him, drawn to the ruckus and entreaties being made by his fallen angels observing Jesus's growing influence and discipleship.

Lucifer himself began to watch more closely what Jesus was doing, listening increasingly to what he was preaching. He tempted Jesus in many ways, trying to impede his divine pilgrimage. He offered repeated temptation, hoping to get Jesus to abandon his mission and join Lucifer in achieving Earth domination. Lucifer did not want to believe Jesus was special, but he also could not be cavalier or careless about it. This intrigue increased immensely once Jesus proclaimed himself as son of the Heavenly Father.

A perplexed, befuddled Lucifer reeled at the notion Jesus was referring to the same Heavenly Father Lucifer had known and served in the celestial realm. He wondered how Jesus could make such a claim. This was compounded by the fact that Jesus (as man) did not remember the heavenly origin of these statements. These anteced-ent heavenly events, however, had become part of Jesus's human ontology.

Jesus sometimes would recollect the words of the old woman who had taught him during his young temple days. Much of what she had imparted to him was frankly hard to believe. She revealed how he would live his life and what would happen to him. He knew in his heart that he had something special to accomplish on Earth, but he didn't know what it was or even who he was. All he did know was that he had to teach. And when he taught, the words and thoughts just came to him. When he healed, he also did not know what hap-pened. Other people had the power to heal too. When Jesus healed, though, a beautiful energy flowed forth from him. Many around him felt its transforming effect.

During the final week of his life, Jesus was placed on a donkey before entering Jerusalem. This was just as the old woman had fore-told. People greeted him like a king because of the many miracles he had performed. They believed he was the "promised one" who would release Israel from its slavery to Rome. Glancing at the worshipping crowds huddled along the pathway into Jerusalem, Jesus recalled the old woman's prophecy: "They will praise you like a king, but they will kill you like a thief."

Lucifer's jealousy toward Jesus reached heights akin to his envy toward the Heavenly Father. He still did not realize fully who Jesus was in the Divine Plan, but he was determined to do whatever neces-sary to stop his being made a king, an earthly ruler not under Lucifer's control. He decided Jesus had to be killed before more of humanity began to worship him.

Exercising his incredible power, Lucifer contorted the think-ing of many minds and hearts among the people. He twisted them against Jesus, instilling in them condemnation and hatred. For all intents and purposes, Jesus was already condemned prior to his being brought before the civil, religious, and Roman authorities for judgment. While there were many in the crowd who objected to the criminal prosecution of Jesus, especially his sentence of death by crucifixion, their fear kept them silent. They were afraid to speak out in his defense.

Later in the week, after entering Jerusalem in triumph, his mother Mary and her sister Martha baked bread for a dinner Jesus wanted to have with his disciples at the home of a friend and follower. Mary told Jesus it would be a simple meal. Jesus asked, "With water, oil, and wine?" Mary responded with a simple yes. She knew what she should do for him even before he asked and understood intimately the symbolism of water as essential for life.

The disciples came one by one to this dinner, save for Judas. As we know, he went first to the Temple to inform the priests where this meal was being held and who would be there. Judas's uncle was on the staff of the Temple. In exchange for this information, intelligence they had been trying to acquire all week, they paid him in silver coins. Demons had entered the hearts and minds of the priests and Judas, spurring on this denunciation of Jesus. His uncle proclaimed proudly to the assembled authorities, a defense of his nephew's actions, "My nephew knows this has to stop." All agreed. Strangely, though, a mixture of sorrow and self-hatred enveloped Judas as the die was cast.

Judas arrived late to the dinner. Jesus greeted him, saying, "You are late, my brother." Judas put his head down. Jesus continued, "Come, sit by me."

John and the other disciples wondered why Jesus gave Judas this honored place at table. Truthfully, they were jealous and bewildered. Hurt feelings encircled the table. The disciples harbored distrust of Judas from the beginning. He was least liked by the eleven other disciples.

When Judas sat down, he could feel the love Jesus had toward him. He did not understand the source of this affection, knowing the wrong he had so recently committed. When he asked to leave the dinner, Jesus placed his hand on his and said, "No, stay with me." Tears began to form in Jesus's eyes because he truly loved Judas as much as his other disciples.

Jesus leaned closer to Judas. He said quietly and privately, "For what you have done, I forgive you." Neither Jesus nor Judas fully understood these words. Judas wondered how Jesus could have known what he had done, though he knew from his discipleship that Jesus seemed to know everything. Jesus had always been very kind to him, defending Judas when other disciples resented or argued with him. Even now Peter and John were hurt by the personal attention Jesus was showing toward Judas.

When the dinner began, Jesus took bread, broke it into pieces, then dipped each piece in the wine. He gave a piece to each of the disciples, one by one. Then he raised his hands in prayer to the Heavenly Father and told his disciples he was sharing his life, his body and blood, with them. After Judas received his piece of bread, he slipped quietly and quickly out of the room. Jesus then took a pitcher and gave each of his disciples a small cup of water.

As the disciples were eating, Jesus leaned over and spoke privately to Little John, the disciple who was so called to distinguish him from the disciple known as Big John. Little John is referred to often as "the disciple Jesus loved." Jesus said quietly to him, "Take care of our mother."

John had heard similar words from his grandfather, Mary's husband Joseph, just before he died. Joseph told him, "I have had another dream. Now I understand much more clearly than before. Mary has been like a mother to you. Her many burdens will be very painful. Be good to her." John began to cry because he wondered what Grandfather Joseph meant by those words.

When super was finished, Jesus said, "Come." They got up and followed him to the Garden of Gethsemane. There he leaned against a large rock and asked them to pray with him. The disciples were bewildered and distraught because Jesus was acting strangely. Tired from a lack of rest, however, one by one they fell asleep. Their spirit was indeed willing, but their flesh weak.

As he prayed alone, Jesus both saw and felt evil. He envisioned his mother crying. With that image burned into his mind and heart, he slipped into a trance. Not knowing what was happening, he fell asleep. When he awoke, a bright light covered the stone. With his hands he wiped his face. When he looked at them he saw blood. He was sweating droplets of blood.

Judas came to the Garden of Gethsemane without being seen. He realized then how much wrong he had done when he saw the blood on Jesus's face. Judas had no idea he had been chosen as part of the Divine Plan for this pivotal role in the plan for humankind's salvation.

Jesus had previously decided to do whatever he was asked to do by the Heavenly Father, without knowing exactly what it might be. Over and over the old woman's voice came back to him. It evoked the terrible things she had predicted would befall him. She had told him these things from the time he was a youth. He even recalled pushing her up against a tree, yelling at her, telling her she was crazy. He did not want to believe what she was saying. Yet, even as he tried to dismiss her premonitions, a part of him knew what she was predicting would come to pass, especially her prophetic words: "You will be treated like a thief and hung on a cross. You will shed your blood and tears before you die."

Unknown to Jesus, that "old woman" was Marguerita in human form.

After Jesus was arrested in the Garden of Gethsemane, he was beaten viciously and shown no mercy. The Roman soldier who beat him had been given extra strength by Lucifer, just so he could inflict enormous pain on Jesus. Jesus also suffered the greatest possible mental and emotional pain. In that condition he had to freely decide if he would be willing to die for our sins and not just suffer for them. That decision had been made in the Garden of Gethsemane, his sweating blood signifying his agreement to accept death.

When they prepared Jesus to be crucified, they first tied ropes around his wrists and feet before a Roman soldier nailed him to a cross. That Roman soldier was Jacobin in human form. He was the only person The One would allow to crucify Jesus.

It had to be done in this way, so his blood would fall upon the Earth. It would later fall on Mary after he was taken down from the Cross and placed in her arms. When the energy from his blood fell on her heart, she knew in her mind that she would return spiritually to Earth to take Marguerita's place in the future. Rose petals represent drops of his blood. That is why apparitions of Mary are often accompanied by the scent of roses.

In agonizing pain Jesus called out from the cross to the Heavenly Father. His Heavenly Father was unable to hear Jesus because a sheath of dark energy had been placed around the crucified Jesus by Lucifer. So encompassing was this shell of darkness, the Heavenly Father was not aware of what was happening on Earth. There was nothing he could do for Jesus. The Heavenly Father had given part of his very being to Lucifer, who still benefited from the love of the Heavenly Father.

Jesus also cried out to Mary and Little John and looked down on them with great sadness and concern. He told them they should look upon one another as mother and son. This was the third time John had heard these words: once from his father, and twice from Jesus. Now he fully understood that he was being asked to watch over Mary. Fortunately, he had already begun doing so after Mary had become part of his extended family.

The Great Father gave additional energy to Jesus so he could tolerate suffering as long as it took to make full amends for the sins of humankind - and do so while continually refusing Lucifer's temptations. Even the Great Father could not take Jesus off the cross as it was all part of the Divine Plan devised by The One. The duration and intensity of Jesus's suffering was measured against the sum total of humankind's sins - past, present, and future. Angels comforted him as best they could while he suffered.

Lucifer enjoyed showing the crucified Jesus how much his mother was suffering. He even promised to take him off the cross and stop his mother's suffering if he would give his life-sustaining energies to him. Jesus spurned these offers no matter how much Lucifer taunted and tempted him in more ways than we can imagine.

He even showed Jesus an image of his entering Jerusalem wearing a glorious robe, sitting on a donkey, moving slowly by adoring crowds who praised him and wanted him to become their king. Jesus dismissed this image from his mind. Jesus knew receiving such praise was wrong because all he had accomplished during his earthly sojourn was done for the Heavenly Father, never for his own edification or self-aggrandizement. This only further infuriated Lucifer. His subjects were paying homage to Jesus, who accepted it begrudgingly. This was homage and adulation Lucifer desired for himself.

While Lucifer was busy tempting Jesus, he failed to realize that Jesus was marking Earth with his blood, sweat, tears, and water. He was doing it so that at the end of time he would return with Mary to take the good souls to Heaven. In doing so, he was also marking every soul who had been created, and would live on Earth, with the same life-giving and loving energy he had fed to the Heavenly Father.

Jesus was barely hanging on to life when a Roman soldier offered him a sponge soaked with vinegar (i.e., sour wine). It was a symbol of what sin had done to humankind. Every aspect of the crucifixion possessed tremendous symbolism. Life had turned sour. Humankind embraced evil. While Jesus's spirit wavered in and out of his mortal body on the cross, Mary also marked Earth with her tears. Her tears would continue to fall upon the Earth long after the crucifixion.

Little John had been one of Mary's favorites among the disciples. He was kind and willing always to help her in any way. She also comforted him when he was ridiculed by others. This ridicule stemmed from John being small in stature, delicate, and, truthfully, feminine in his manner. John had helped Mary in many significant ways before, and after, the death of Jesus. Mary would, for example, send him to find out what Jesus was doing once his ministry had begun. She yearned to know how Jesus was feeling as he crisscrossed the countryside spreading the gospel. John accompanied Mary to the Last Supper. These are only a few of the many reasons why Jesus loved John so much. Lucifer, however, thought of John as completely insignificant. Another example of Lucifer's ego obscuring the truth before him.

John's mother had died giving birth to him. He was raised by a brother and sister until he went to help Joseph, his grandfather, after Joseph brought Mary to live with him in his home. Joseph had five or six children, more girls than boys. John was the youngest child of one of those girls, and he was not full-term when born. He was slightly older than Jesus.

Led by divine light, John took Mary to another country after the death of Jesus because he feared the authorities might seek to kill her as well. Mary spent her remaining years blaming herself for Jesus's death, as only a mother would do. John cared for Mary all the years until her own death. Despite all that she had seen, witnessed, and been part of, she did not fully understand that Jesus was the son of the Heavenly Father until she returned to Heaven.

When Jesus died on the cross, Lucifer became enraged. His anger stemmed from Jesus's refusal to accede to Lucifer's offers of intervention, to recruit him to the ranks of the fallen angels. Lucifer was astounded at Jesus's willingness to withstand the tremendous pain and suffering being meted out during the crucifixion. This dismay stemmed from his being prevented from knowing Jesus's true identity.

The immediate result of the crucifixion for humankind was this: choosing to love and follow the Heavenly Father on Earth now expands to the choice of whether or not to love and follow Jesus and Mary.

Lucifer did not realize fully the momentousness of the crucifixion because he was enraged from failing to convince Jesus to give his life to him. Recognition of the profundity of the crucifixion and its intrinsic threat to his kingdom occurred only after Jesus died. It was then Lucifer heard Jesus say to him subconsciously, yet directly, "I have marked the Earth. It is mine." If Jesus had not claimed the Earth, every soul would have been lost.

After he died on the cross, a band of angels, including his own guardian angel, accompanied by the archangel of death, carried his spirit straight away to the Heavenly Father. These were the same angels whose supply of loving and compassionate energy, along with energy coming from the Great Father, allowed Jesus to endure on the cross for as long as he did. Jesus could not have died sooner, because redeeming the tremendous sins of all humanity required lengthy agony and extreme purgation. On his way home again to Heaven, he established a trail of tears across the universe.

Only upon his return to Heaven did he and Mary understand truly and fully who he was and what he had accomplished in his earthly mission. Jesus was greeted with great joy and love by the Heavenly Host. It was then Jesus remembered all that had happened in Heaven before he and Mary had descended to Earth. His integral connection with Mary triggered great sorrow and pain, preparation for what she was about to experience on Earth.

In his reunion with the Heavenly Father, Jesus heard him say, "You have marked the Earth with all you have shed. I could not take you off the cross." Jesus replied, "I gave everything I had for the sins of the world. Have mercy on all those who have lived on Earth in the past, now, and in the future."

If Jesus had not died on the cross, every soul would have been lost. Lucifer would have prevailed. He believed he would have made Earth, and everyone on it his, free to do with us whatever he desired, inflicting pain on each of us as Jesus had suffered. But it was not, and is not, the Divine Plan. Salvation is ours.

The Heavenly Father's ebullience at Jesus's homecoming stemmed from the fulfillment of the mission he had been sent to Earth to accomplish, but also because Jesus again fed the Heavenly Father with purer and stronger energy than ever before. This energy made the Heavenly Father feel better than he had since those first cherished days with Lucifer.

Lucifer, though, was infuriated by Jesus's return to Heaven, especially knowing Jesus had assumed the exalted position Lucifer had once held. He sought revenge against the good angels who had been sent to Earth to counterbalance his earthly dominance. Fortunately, he did not have the power to exact this retribution.

Today, and for the rest of time, Jesus weeps for all those on Earth. He considers us to be his adopted children from the Heavenly Father. His love is greater than any gift one could ever possibly receive. It strengthens all life on Earth, including the good angels who stand guard before the vortexes. They are waiting relentlessly for the rise of demons, forcing them to see the evil they are spreading all over the Earth. This battle of wills between good angels and demons persists every moment of every day.

Jesus now knows much more about the structure of the universe than he did before he left Heaven. He also better understands the role of the Great Father and Marguerita from whom he and Mary received life. He wants to help us live our lives according to the commandments of the Heavenly Father, who will continue to supply us with life-sustaining energy until the end of the world.

While on Earth, Mary's heart had often been pierced by pain and sorrow. It happened when Jesus was born, when he left her to begin his ministry, and, of course, when he died on the cross. Her suffering was shared sacrifice born likewise for the sins of humanity. This suffering gave her more energy and strength to do God's will. Her tears helped mark the Earth for Jesus.

When Marguerita's human form leaves Earth after her last life, her departure will enable Mary to appear more often to her children so she can bring them away from Lucifer and back to the Heavenly Father. Mary will spread Marguerita's words like tears throughout the universe so as to cleanse Earth from the blood that has been shed needlessly. The energy of those bloodstains will remain until the final destruction of Earth.

When Mary died, energy from her spirit could be seen as she was taken up into Heaven, just as was Jesus. They both received special sacred energy upon their return to Heaven. Jesus was declared to be the Son of God by a special kind of divine metamorphosis because of his faithfulness to the Divine Plan.

Jesus and Mary know that evil is spreading rapidly throughout the Earth despite their heartfelt efforts. Therefore they cry out to both the Heavenly Father and the Great Father to help us in our struggles. The Heavenly Father was chosen by The One to serve as our God. The Heavenly Father, who has endured his own share of heart wrenching struggles on our behalf, understands and loves us more than we can imagine. In that respect we can truly be said to be the children of God as he too has known great sadness, disappointment, and of feeling abandoned.

While the Heavenly Father was unaware of what was happening in Heaven or on Earth, the Great Father cared for us, answering our prayers. The angels carried these prayers first to the Heavenly Father and then to the all-knowing and all-powerful Great Father.

When you make the sign of the cross on yourself, physically or mentally, it is a protective covering of grace. Lucifer is troubled deeply when we make it as it reminds him of all that had, and had not, happened on the cross. He not only recollects and hears the reenactment of Jesus's death but is reminded vividly of what he personally lost when he was cut from Heaven.

Lucifer feels sorry for himself, an angry, bitter specter. He becomes infuriated when the Sacred Host is elevated during the Sacrifice of the Mass. He views the Catholic Church as his archenemy and has vowed to destroy it in many ways, but especially by infiltrating its leadership at every level. Need we go into detail about the trials and tribulations evil has brought to the Church in our own lifetime?

There is still reason to hope, despite our world being riled by so much evil. Much of that hope stems from the revelations in this book about the origins of Lucifer, his selfish, egomaniacal ways, and the wholehearted desire of the Heavenly Father to not only receive our love but also to return it to us many times over. A life sustained by sacred love, the most powerful of all energies, is the precious gift we have received from the Heavenly Father. This gift is our precious endowment, a dowry of love from above. It is a gift that, ironically, increases the more we give it away to others, similar to Jesus feeding thousands of followers from a meager offering of five loaves of bread and two fish.

The renewed energy of the Heavenly Father is reflected in the rainbow of colors emanating from the archangels surrounding him. His four brothers are surprised by this reinvigoration, but very pleased to discover who their brother truly is at last. They are thrilled to see him finally assuming the role in the universe for which he was intended. To help him in this resurgence, they are sending some of their best followers to help humans overcome evil throughout the world.

The Heavenly Father is not resting nowadays nearly as often as he needed to rest in the past. Much of his original energy is being renewed and restored, but not all of it. It is Marguerita who has opened the flow of pure energy to him. The two groups of three bands of archangels surrounding the Heavenly Father are gravitating ever closer to him, providing him with that energy. It is time for that to happen. Each band of archangels previously emitted different colors. Now their intermingling with one another results in a bright, beautiful rainbow.

Jacobin/Michael is also helping to revitalize the Heavenly Father's awareness. Marguerita is guiding Michael when he is in Heaven and Jacobin when he is on Earth. Three large bands of archangels will protect Jacobin in the many lives he still must live on Earth. Their sole charge is to make certain he can accomplish what he was sent to do.

It was humanity's prayers and petitions to the Heavenly Father that sustained him during the energy starvation orchestrated by Lucifer. "Prayerful angels" carried these sources of loving energy to the Heavenly Father, then onward to the Great Father. The Great Father further enriched them and provided them to the Heavenly Father. All prayers directed to "God," regardless of religion, are taken to the Heavenly Father.

Love has the power, the creative energy, to cleanse and heal us in life. That is why newborns are given a special gift of love from the Heavenly Father when they are conceived. He wants them to help rid Earth of its many evils and destructive tendencies. Prayers and blessings are important spiritual weapons in this effort. They manifest powerful energy that can give hope when evil seems to be in control. The Heavenly Father has created each and every one of us to do great works with this seemingly simple gift called prayer.

Lucifer has always laughed loudly at those who pray. He believes they are wasting their time, as evidenced by the power he exerts all over the globe. When a mother longs for a lost child and feels no consolation coming from her God, Lucifer feels triumphant. He readily mocks the Heavenly Father. His evil, however, may have been too successful. More and more people all around Earth are crying out to the Heavenly Father for mercy and his loving intervention. Lucifer can see how this torrent of prayer is giving the Heavenly Father strength and renewal. This has muffled Lucifer's boasting significantly.

What bothers Lucifer the most are prayers offered for those who have died, especially prayers offered in union with the death of Jesus on the cross, as those offered during every Mass. These prayers not only force him to remember what Jesus achieved on Calvary, but these heartfelt petitions receive even greater power and prominence when they are joined to the crucified Jesus. Jesus on the cross joins with us when we cry out to the Heavenly Father. Our prayerful pleading becomes echoed and multiplied with our Crucified Savior. All prayer stands as a very powerful life force elixir. We need them always, especially in the transition from one life to the next.

Jesus as *Lumen Gentium* (Light of the World) confirms the concept of three entities existing as one indivisible deity. Understanding and accepting the Trinity is of utmost importance to all. It can help us begin to understand how and why different types of energy are needed to create, sustain, renew, and guide life. This truth has been innate human comprehension from our very origins. It is reflected in both the simple and complex: from Native American tepees to the great pyramids of Egypt and Mesoamerica. Such triangles of power, love, and truth exist across myriad cultures.

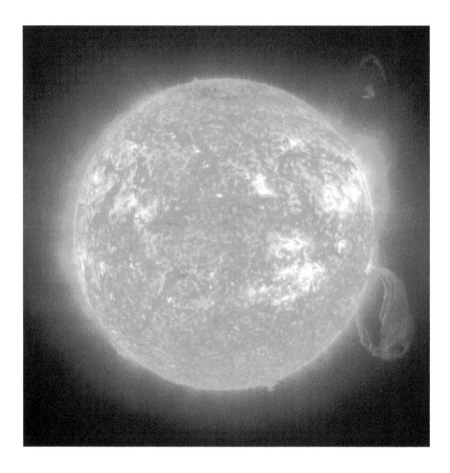

At the appointed time, Mother Nature will
cause the sun to hurdle toward Earth.

End Times

According to the Divine Plan, Lucifer has been given only so much time to reign over the Earth before it will be destroyed. Eternity exists only in Heaven; Earth was never created to last forever. This is because it is, frankly, imperfect.

While he was creating it, the Heavenly Father needed to rest for seven long epochs - the "days" mentioned in the Bible. It was necessary for him to stop, renew, and restore his strength during each hiatus because Lucifer was taking so much energy from him at the same time. This lack of constant attention to creation of the Earth weakened integral parts of its composition and structure.

Another factor contributing to its weakness was the haste with which the Heavenly Father created Earth as Lucifer's kingdom. This rush occurred because the Heavenly Father needed a place for Lucifer to occupy once he was cut forcibly from Heaven. An even greater factor is that Earth was not created with the same energy used to create the other planets. These and other factors contributed to Earth's overall vulnerability.

Lucifer does not believe what has been revealed herein, especially the prophecy that there will soon be a period when he will be bound on Earth by Marguerita. During that fateful time, the Great Father will send an army of angels to Earth. They will descend to

Earth precisely when the division between good and evil becomes critical. These angels will force the demons to acknowledge what Lucifer is doing and what he has become.

Marguerita absorbs Lucifer's anger so she can better understand him. This understanding will prove instrumental when Marguerita undertakes another action demanded of her by the Divine Plan: she will bind and neutralize Lucifer, but only to unleash even more evil on Earth.

When Marguerita binds Lucifer, there will be peace on Earth for a designated duration of time according to the Divine Plan. At first the demons will not realize what has happened to Lucifer. When they understand Lucifer has been suddenly neutralized, there will be havoc on Earth. The fallen angels will not listen to one another. They will seek to cause as much evil among humanity as possible. It will be a bacchanalia of satanic anarchy.

When Lucifer is finally released from Marguerita, he will use his unspent, torpid energy to create greater evil than had ever existed. The only good that will come from this vile epoch will be people calling out ever more frequently and fervently to the Heavenly Father for mercy. Souls should seek such mercy for themselves; the world itself will remain wracked by evil until the end of time. Unless we change our ways, evil will accelerate and there will be even greater problems on Earth, a planet that has been partially off its axis from its very origin.

In these end times we can expect Lucifer's attacks on the Church to be greater than ever. He will make every effort to destroy the Church, because unlike other worldly institutions, it alone has the power to overcome evil. While he will not be totally successful, he will inflict great damage on the bride of Christ.

Marguerita will not be able to do anything to stop him. She must go into a period of rest. During this parasomnia, she will watch Earth's ultimate demise and the judgment of all. In most respects, her mission will have been accomplished. She will have already taught us that the most valuable lesson we can learn is that love fosters love and truth fosters truth. Each of us has been given a spiritual key that can open our mind, heart, and soul to truths that will be revealed to us because of our love for God, angels, humankind, animals, and nature.

It will now be time for Jacobin/Michael to act.

The destruction of Earth, the ultimate demise of Lucifer's kingdom, will occur in much less than the blink of an eye. The same loud, terrifying sound heard on Earth when Jesus died on the cross will be heard again for one final time. Lucifer will remember it when he hears it. He will also hear within himself the voice of Jesus, who said to him as he died on the cross: "I have marked the Earth. It is mine."

At that moment, Lucifer will cry out a loud death rattle. The realization that he has lost almost all his energy, his very *raison d'être*, and that the end is neigh will reveal a shattered, bitter creature. He will have grown much weaker, unable to contain the evil energy burning within him. He will realize for the first time that he has lost everything. His demons will no longer be able to provide him with the energy needed to sustain existence. This burning within him, especially in his eyes, has been seen by some humans. They describe it, rightfully, as the "fires of hell."

The time will come when Earth will have very little goodness remaining in it. Evil will have grown and spread rapidly like a mold or virus coming forth from Lucifer. Human beings will be filled with so much sin and evil they will have forfeited any chance of being renewed by the Heavenly Father at life's end. Humans will only be able to carry evil with them from Earth to Heaven and back, a fruitless cycle doomed to failure.

In Earth's last moments, Mother Nature will call out in great anger because of the terrible destruction humans caused to her creation. She will know the moment for final judgment has arrived and will begin the process of destroying and renewing Earth at the same precise time.

Her powerful energy will cause the sun to spin very quickly and pick up great centrifugal force before it hurdles violently toward the Earth at incredible speed. Recall the miracle of the Sun at Fatima. A preview, perhaps, of this very end time. As it hits Earth, all life will be destroyed completely. The exploding vortexes will contribute to this total destruction, then the planet itself will be cleansed of all vestiges of human existence. Everyone who has ever lived will have returned from living on other planets or from being at rest waiting for this final judgment.

With a tear falling upon it from Mother Nature, the cleansed Earth will be wonderfully restored to the original beauty that had been intended. Then, with great empathy, Marguerita will give Earth back to Mother Nature before it dissolves into an invisible energy force. All these events will happen in a single instant, but they will bring with them great love and joy to Mother Nature.

All human souls will be judged in that one shining moment. They will proceed immediately to either Jesus and Mary or Lucifer. The final judgment will be the result of the choices we have made throughout all our earthly lives. In that same moment we will transform into the same spirit form in which we had first been created and placed on Earth.

The angels and human beings who chose to follow Lucifer will be drawn to him; the angels and humans who followed the ways of the Heavenly Father will be drawn to Jesus and Mary. In a final battle of wills, the good angels will force the demons to see all the evil they have committed. The truest definition of hell.

Jacobin will appear suddenly as the beautiful and powerful archangel Michael. In his hand he will hold a source of pure energy shaped like a sword. This triumphant sword is the handiwork of the Great Father and John Andrew. John Andrew is part angel, part human but is infused with power coming directly from The One. There is no creature like John Andrew in the universe. He is a huge, unique ball of pure energy domiciled in Heaven. His task is to keep everything in balance. John Andrew, the offspring of Jacobin and Marguerita, will be the one to hand the sword to Michael.

Before Michael cuts Lucifer, he will stare him down. As Lucifer crumbles before him, Michael will proclaim, "My brother." These words will open the mind of Lucifer fully to all that he has destroyed. This is when Lucifer will wholly feel the pain he has caused throughout Earth's existence. He will be inundated with the pent-up cries not only of all those who were killed on Earth, but also the wailing cries of demons baffled by all that is happening to them as Lucifer's realm implodes. In dismay they will bemoan, "We followed you. We followed you! Why?"

A part of the energy constituting this sword will come from angels who view Michael as their brother. They realize the difficulty he may have in cutting the final two intertwined cords of a heavenly being who was very much a brother to him. The first cut was made when Lucifer was expelled to Earth. Now, with one final blow, Michael will cut completely the lifeline from which Lucifer continued to receive energy from the Heavenly Father. The last line of communication between Lucifer and the Heavenly Father, barely used of late, will finally be severed.

This sword of Armageddon resonates with the cries of those whose blood has been shed unjustly throughout the history of Earth. Appropriately, when Lucifer is finally cut, he will send forth a bloodcurdling scream. It will be a scream equivalent to the one he unleashed falling from Heaven. The trauma of this cataclysm will result in both Lucifer and the Heavenly Father falling into deep sleep simultaneously. The Heavenly Father will be attended by his angelic hosts; Lucifer will dwell in solitary darkness.

When Michael makes the final cut, he will do it with love for his brother Lucifer but he will also be doing it for the well-being of those now joined to Jesus and Mary. Justice will have prevailed. This cut will leave Lucifer looking like he has two horns on his head, stumps of the final two cords to the Heavenly Father. He will also drag behind him what we would describe as a tail, though in actuality that is the remnant of the first cord cut by the Great Father and Marguerita precipitating Lucifer's fall from Heaven to Earth.

The souls who have given their lives to Lucifer will realize in agony the wrong they have done. These distressed creatures will understand at last the harm they have caused themselves as a result of choosing Lucifer through their free will. They will orbit the empty space where Earth once existed. Jesus and Mary, and their followers, will circle closer to the energy force; but they will be unseen by Lucifer's legions by a blanket of love placed over them by Jesus and Mary.

The guardian angels of souls on Earth who were drawn to Jesus and Mary will remain with them. The guardian angels of souls who were drawn to Lucifer will be sent to a place of rest because they weren't totally responsible for the decisions of human souls who ignored them and chose the Evil One.

Much later, and no one knows how long, all life will return to The One. The good souls will pass by first, then follow Him, the Supreme Creator, the Golden Light, the Great Father, the Supreme Being, and the Source of All Life into a state of rest and renewal. Finally, the souls who turned away from the Heavenly Father and pledged themselves to Lucifer will follow him into the golden light - where they will be judged again. Marguerita and Jacobin will make the preparations for this event when it is time. They will return later.

Lucifer will be judged harshly. He will suffer most when he sees the bloodshed he has spread over the entire Earth. He will be the only part of creation to be destroyed completely. His remaining energy will be dispersed throughout the universe. As divine poetic justice, no harm will be caused to any other living creature by the remnants of Lucifer's energy.

At that time, as far as we can tell, the Divine Plan for this universe will be complete. It is a plan beyond human understanding, despite all that has been revealed. Only the Wisdom within the Divine Plan will determine when more mysteries will be revealed. Rest assured, many remain.

The pyramids of Egypt are the finest example
of an infusion of alien intelligence.

Credit: cinoby

THE EIGHTH CHAPTER

Other Life in the Universe

The first four sons of the Great Father have been watching closely events unfolding on Earth from its conception. They were also watching how their brother, the Heavenly Father, was being affected by those changes. It was out of great concern that they shared some of their own life forces to help him in his development. In the beginning, these four Brothers had also given some of their cumulative energy to Lucifer to assist him in caring for their younger brother.

Lucifer misused the energy they had given him. A combination of resentment and anger now fuels their attitude toward Lucifer. If it were possible, the four Brothers would destroy him now but The One will not allow it. As a result, the Brothers consistently teased Lucifer. They emphasized how much stronger they were than he, how much better their individual kingdoms were than his. They referred to the evil and destruction happening on Earth.

It was the Golden Light who inspired the Brothers to send their subjects to Earth. Consequently, each of the Brothers opted to send their respective followers to Earth to discover what had gone wrong, why it had, and what might be done to improve it. Wanting to experience it firsthand, they designed and built spaceships to protect these explorers from the harsh atmosphere of Earth. Our atmosphere readily sustains human life but is not necessarily conducive to alien beings.

These subjects had the ability to travel spiritually, but in order to interact with humans in similar corporeal form, they needed to adopt humanlike physiques. Each Brother had originally sent explorers and researchers to Earth separately, albeit unknown to each other. Of late, however, they have become aware of their shared concern and interest in Earth.

The eldest was first to send subjects to Earth, followed shortly thereafter by the second brother. Brothers three and four soon followed. Since the Brothers are spiritual beings, they can only be seen on Earth when they choose to project themselves in humanlike form.

At first they considered their fifth and younger brother, our Heavenly Father, as a kind of misfit. They believed he wasn't strong enough to deal with the recalcitrant and thieving Lucifer who had stolen a great deal of energy from the Heavenly Father. They blamed their brother for Earth's wayward, seemingly rudderless, direction. It was hoped these vanguard explorers could restore the peace that had existed between humans, animals, angels, and Mother Nature at the beginning of creation. At first the Brothers took only animals from Earth, not humans. They were curious as to how a spirit could become animal-like.

The Brothers then began to covet human beings. They were curious about what humans believed, how these beliefs influenced and changed their behavior. They also wanted to know about human emotions. Followers of the Brothers do not experience human affectations such as agony, hurt, physical discomfort. Consequently, they do not understand the human experience of pain. Of special fascination to the four Brothers was the distinctly human concept of free will and how it seemed to so drastically change the direction of life on Earth.

After examining the best and worst of what they found on Earth, the Brothers brought both humans and animals back to their home planets to experiment on them. This action violated fundamentally the Divine Plan. It was wrong. Especially heinous was using these innocents as "specimens." The energy given by the Great Father was to have been used only to promote good in their own kingdoms, not to actively intercede in other worlds.

The four Brothers tried unsuccessfully to infuse our DNA into their own spiritual beings. Their scavenging of Earth led to the demise of animals and humans on their home planets, oftentimes as a result of experimentation. These deceased creatures exist now in spirit form, as they were at life's beginning, but on their own planet.

The Great Father has since commanded the return of these abducted specimens. He ordered the four brothers to return prehistoric creatures, extinct animals, and other unique life-forms back to Earth. Expect to see in the not-too-distant future inimitable creatures reappearing in isolated places on our planet.

Some of these humans and animals have already returned to Earth. One prime example is the creature we refer to as Big Foot or Sasquatch. These creatures exist. They are male and female humans who were taken away from Earth at a specific stage of development, essentially antecedents of the humans we have become. There are actually four or five strains of Big Foot/Sasquatch, each marking a stage of development when hominids began to eat animals.

The offspring of the physical animals being brought back to Earth will mutate and procreate over time, creating species never seen before. This will cause many problems regarding environmental balance. Our initial reaction may be the desire to eradicate them, but we should not.

The superior intelligence of the four brothers gave human beings additional energy to further develop our brains. Injection of superior intelligence resulted in the building of the great monuments throughout the ancient world. The pyramids of Egypt are arguably the finest example of this infusion of alien intelligence. The purpose of the pyramids was to pull down energy to strengthen Earth, to remind humankind we are not alone, that power much greater than our own exists in other worlds throughout the universe. Various images of Lucifer within ancient writings will be found within inner secret chambers of the pyramids as further proof of his existence and all he has done to our world. These pyramids, as well as many other archaeological monuments and formations scattered across the Earth, serve as guidepost for the Brothers' subjects when they visit Earth.

When humans began to build images of Lucifer as a medium of deistic worship, Brothers three and four urged them to select their own leaders on Earth, rather than allow Lucifer to control them. It was the beginning of humankind taking charge of its own destiny.

Some of the followers took energy from animals that had been placed on Earth before humans arrived. They did this at the urging of Lucifer, who instilled in them the mistaken belief that absorbing these energies would replicate his own beauty and power. Lucifer lusted for some of this different energy, hoping it would allow him to break through the barrier preventing him from rejoining the Heavenly Father again. He even tries to influence the Brothers to side with him so he can use their energy for sustenance. Marguerita, as we have reiterated repeatedly, will never allow it.

These same Brothers were partially responsible for some humans worshipping Lucifer. The brothers created great storms on Earth as a way of punishing those who followed Lucifer. The opposite reaction occurred. These storms drove many on Earth to embrace Lucifer's antipathy toward the Heavenly Father because they were terrified at what was happening. They thought the Heavenly Father had either caused storms or had lost his power to prevent them. We see this thought process at work today whenever a cataclysm occurs around the world.

Some of the Brothers' subjects perished here from Earth's pollution. Fact is, some of these alien bodies have indeed been recovered while more will be unearthed in the future. We have experimented on some of these bodies, in the same way they have experimented on us. Without realizing it, some of them were still alive. We inflicted great pain on them. As a result, we have become their enemy.

We inhabitants of Earth are viewed by some of the Brother's followers as galactic "trash" and/or "primitive beings." Some believe we should be eradicated entirely. That is due to the Brothers not having full control over their subjects. Many followers are motivated by a desire to help the fallen angels, believing they did not have full knowledge of what they were doing during the great cataclysm that upset the celestial realm. The Great Father and Marguerita will not permit this to happen. Fortunately, the Brothers' greatest desire is for human beings to come back to the Heavenly Father, to recognize this supernatural majesty once again as our "God."

The Brothers want us to know there is a God, who is The One, a God who will seek justice for humankind's evil behavior. Although the subjects of the four Brothers have lived and worked among us for ages, they are unable to procreate. Some of the Brother's followers projected themselves at various times on Earth in partial animal form. This is why they were believed to be gods by earthlings due to the fantastic powers they possessed and demonstrated. The Brothers used these powers to astonish humans in hopes of changing their wayward behavior.

Marguerita transmitted to the four Brothers' additional energy to allow them to send "experts" from among their subjects to assist humans in the struggle against evil. Now that they have a better understanding of their Brother, the Heavenly Father, they have become more compassionate toward him.

The pantheon of celestial beings influencing our Earth extends well beyond the Heavenly Father's four Brothers and their subjects (i.e., our aliens). It is necessary for us to turn back time to Lucifer's initial banishment to Earth and the four archangels that followed him. These were very powerful archangels. So powerful they were able to release some of their heaven-born energy in the formation of additional angels. They were also able to project themselves into human form.

These newly formed angels began to covet female human beings who had evolved from spiritual to physical form. This transformation occurred when humans chose not to live according to the Heavenly Father's commandments. A major transgression was humankind drawing energy from animals. This began while both were still in a spiritual state and continued as they evolved into physical form.

These young angels wanted to be like human beings who had begun to use their mental capacity in limited, often unclear, ways. In their effort to become more like them, these angels forced their spiritual energy into the bodies of females all over Earth. This was not physical union as we know it, but rather a uniting of spiritual and physical energy. Sexual organs weren't necessary; conception occurred solely through the power of mind.

Males were created to be both protector and provider for the family unit. By their very nature, females were not as strong as males. This was due solely to females having been created after males, with a lesser, different kind of energy. Male and female energies are distinct. Each has been given special gifts. Truth be told, in the Divine Plan, females are more important than males.

The offspring conceived in these chosen women produced a new species of angel. So large was their physique most women died giving birth, some in gestation. These new beings did not have a formal name, though they are referenced in the Bible. When the amount of energy needed to create these children diminished, these newly conceived beings became much smaller, and mostly male at birth.

The women who died giving birth to these beings were forced to return to the Heavenly Father to be renewed sooner than their designated times. This change dramatically affected the plan established for the spiritual renewal of the human race. By influencing these angels to procreate, Lucifer was able to throw the natural birth process out of balance. He wanted to show the Heavenly Father the extent to which his earthly creations had so readily morphed into evil ways. It was Lucifer's way of proclaiming, "See how powerful I am! Look at what you have done wrong!"

The newly created beings grew to hate one another. Battles broke out between them. Most humans feared these creatures because they were very strange and harmful to humans. For example, when one sneezed, they spewed forth negative energy affecting the minds of humans. When they said, "God bless you," they meant it. Animosity and antagonism developed to the point that this new species and humans began to kill each other. Humans would prove triumphant in this struggle, though the energy of these defeated hybrid creatures remain in various locales on Earth. There they emit a dark, permanent energy of hatred affecting all who approach. Skeletons of this extinct race will be found in the future.

The good angels who were sent to Earth with the initial seeds of life still remain. They stand forthright before the fallen angels and engage them in a battle of wits. The fallen angels retain free reign to do what they want with the powerful energy they possess. The good angels, however, seek to frustrate the fallen angel's nefarious intent with humans. The mind of an angel is different from that of a human or animal. It is a "weapon" used to influence what human beings think, believe, and, consequently, how they behave. It can trigger in humans either inspiration or temptation. Such is the duel between the good and fallen angels.

At the beginning of life on Earth, the Heavenly Father believed the angels in Heaven, combined with the angels who had followed Lucifer, would inspire human beings positively to do what was right and just. He thought both groups would be a source of blessing in Lucifer's kingdom, inspiring humans to behave in accordance with his commandments. He was mistaken. Even today, a chastened Lucifer, recognizing the precarious nature of Earth, begs the Brothers to open the gates of Heaven to him. This will never happen.

The Heavenly Father did not realize that the great energy of brilliant white, uncreated light emanating from the three bands of archangels surrounding him, was sentient and fully alive. This is the Holy Spirit. The Holy Spirit is a divine source of inspiration and the most powerful source of energy emanating from The One. Ironically, even this mighty force cannot completely overcome sin, because it is unable to negate the gift of free will granted to humans by the Heavenly Father.

The Holy Spirit entered our universe on a spiritual path prepared by Marguerita. Marguerita conceived and formulated this pilgrimage during gestation of the celestial beings. The One provided the energy of the Holy Spirit to protect and sustain the Heavenly Father—that is, until Lucifer was created to balance him. The power of the Holy Spirit radiating from the three bands of archangels did not become fully active until Jesus died on the cross. At the end of time Jesus will draw from this Holy Spirit of Love divine protection. He will disseminate it to those who have chosen to follow Jesus and Mary.

The Holy Spirit maintains balance as part of a Trinity with the Heavenly Father and Jesus. When Jesus was sent to Earth, the Holy Spirit sustained the Heavenly Father while awaiting Jesus's triumphant return. The Holy Spirit will also strengthen Michael for what he must do at the end of the world. For while Marguerita and Michael dwell on Earth, the Holy Spirit's life force and radiant energy is greater than theirs.

Lumen Gentium is a portal for angels
transitioning between heaven and Earth.

This image is owned by Monsignor Ron
and was done by Lou Astorino.

Lumen Gentium as a Living Legacy

A major impetus of Vatican II was reinvigoration of the original missionary nature of the Church. This pillar of the Church was emphasized further by the dogmatic constitution of *Lumen Gentium*. By calling it Lumen Gentium, a Latin phrase literally meaning "light of all nations," the aim was to make manifest the Second Vatican Council's Constitution on the Mystery of the Church proclaiming Christ as the "light of the world."

In this inspired treatise, the Church was defined as "the sacrament...of the unity of the human race." And through this, to make manifest the words of *1 Corinthians 12:13*: "For in one Spirit we were all baptized into one body, whether Jews or Greeks, slave or free, and we were all given one Spirit to drink." This charge to be the symbol of ecumenism, interfaith dialogue, and a forum for reconciliation aims to unite humanity rather than divide it.

It is recognized colloquially and spiritually that all things must come to an end. As we have seen in this revelation, there is undoubtedly a Divine Plan culminating ultimately in the transformation of all things on Earth back to their perfect spiritual form.

We are, though, beings-in-time. Our lives on Earth may be short or long, but earthly incarnation has purpose. The insights and revelations contained in this work highlight responsibilities human beings have in seeking to overcome the failings and shortcomings necessitating each soul's return to corporeal existence.

One very specific revelation given is the Heavenly Father's desire for creation of a material structure manifesting physically the spirit of Lumen Gentium. This facility is to be an ecumenical and interfaith center unlike any ever created before. It is to serve as a pilgrimage site; a place of reflection, reconciliation, spiritual recompense, problem-solving; a sanctuary of peace, self-reflection, excitement, enlightenment, and vitality.

In keeping with Christ's repeated admonitions to proclaim the good news to all peoples across the globe, the physical Lumen Gentium seeks to merge all aspects of human ontology with corresponding manifestations of hope and transcendent aspiration.

And it is ordained that this worldly, physical Lumen Gentium be built in Pittsburgh, Pennsylvania, standing as a beacon of faith and hope for the people of Pittsburgh, Southwestern Pennsylvania, the country, truly, for the entire world. Anglicans, Catholics, Orthodox, Protestants, and those from other faith communities, including Jews, Muslims and Hindus, believe Pittsburgh to be a holy place.

The religious faith of the people in Pittsburgh's many distinctive, ethnic neighborhoods has helped Pittsburgh be recognized repeatedly as America's Most Livable City. That faith remains one of the region's most precious gifts, motivating us to understand, appreciate, and respect one another ever more deeply.

As we have seen throughout this revelation, The One works in trinities. Pittsburgh's three rivers, a veritable aquatic trinity, identify it as a special place. The Allegheny flows down from the north; the Monongahela comes in from the south. They converge at Pittsburgh's point to create the mighty Ohio, which flows west until it merges with the Mississippi River on its way to the Gulf of Mexico and the world's oceans. Each of these rivers possesses its own mystery and magic from their pure mountain origins to the way they flow.

Spiritually, this region of Earth provided great comfort to the Heavenly Father. After he had created Earth in the form of a ball of energy provided to him by the Great Father and his Brothers, it still was not strong enough. Additional celestial energy entered the Earth at the spot where Pittsburgh is located, making it the most sacred spot on Earth. It was on that same spot that the Heavenly Father's "tears" fell when he thought about Lucifer leaving him. These combined with the tears from angels who wept for the Heavenly Father in his sorrow.

Pittsburgh has been protected by its three rivers and by its many hills or mountains whose stones and rocks deflect evil energy, but also by a fourth unknown, hidden river—not the aquifer—that runs deep with the earth, but which will one day rise to the surface. Additional protection came for many decades from the smoke and fire of its steel mills. Lucifer left Pittsburgh alone because its mocking as "hell with the lid off" actually provided him with comfort. Lumen Gentium will provide that same level of protection, protection we will need even more once it is built.

The Heavenly Father's energy helped form the rivers; his human children helped tame them. This convergence of rivers, valleys, hills, pastoral landscapes, mornings, sunsets, and its supernal history accentuate it as the most sacred spot on Earth.

The importance of this is that the Heavenly Father has decreed the physical Lumen Gentium to be built near water, preferably flowing water. This flowing water symbolizes both the tears shed by angels throughout eternity and the precious water that flowed from the side of Jesus on the cross.

The material structure and internal artistry of the physical Lumen Gentium is also to be a celebration of humankind's intellectual transformation made manifest and pronounced in humanity's technological evolution. There has been a shocking misunderstanding regarding the spiritual dynamics of humanity's technological growth. We need to see beyond the individual trees of technological development to the larger forest of how it manifests and highlights human evolution.

The distancing of technology from art and spirituality is to be rent asunder in the Lumen Gentium vision. Reflecting upon the astounding evolution of technology over the last few decades reveals an ever-increasing imitation and aspiration of and for divine attributes. Generally accepted divine attributes include omnipresence, omnipotence, omniscience, and eternal existence.

Humankind, in its unending quest to become like God, has created technologies aspiring to these divine attributes - whether it realizes it or not. Think about the Internet. The Internet's ultimate goal is worldwide connectivity, the desire - and ability - to communicate and interact with anyone anywhere. The phrase used by technologists in describing this capability is "real time." "Real time" accentuates the omnipresence afforded by this technology; it is humankind's attempt to overcome the restraints and restrictions of time. In the same way that God is everywhere, humankind likewise aspires for this same omnipresence. The Internet never sleeps, neither does The One.

Another example of deistic ambition can be seen in something as simple as Wikipedia, Nupedia, Citizendium, and other website repositories of knowledge. Humankind has reached the point where unknowing can be changed into knowing quickly and easily. "Seek and ye shall find/Ask and ye shall receive" is manifested simplistically (but effectively) by the Amazon Alexa, Google Home, Apple HomePod, or other similar technologies. The handicap on unknowing is being addressed head-on by technology. We even refer to the repository of this knowledge as residing in the "cloud." Of course, these bits of data are not levitating in cumulus-nimbus cloud formations but reside instead on thousands of computer hard drives. We reference the "cloud" for its metaphoric connotation. Technically, it refers to the "cloud drawing" used in the past to represent diagrammatically complex communication networks. Serendipity, however, also makes it connote the dwelling place of the supernatural. An intriguing coincidence.

Adding perceptions of omnipresence and omniscience together has given much of humankind a taste of omnipotence. Knowledge as power has been transformational in fields such as medicine, healthcare, physics, manufacturing, chemistry, and more.

These amazing technological transformations, however, have not gotten humanity any closer to the supreme deistic attributes of omnibenevolence or the ultimate deistic attribute: love. In fact, as with all things within the earthly plain, humankind's deistic aspiration has been hijacked oftentimes by Satan. The result of which has been digital viruses, malware, ransomware, weapons of mass destruction, and ever-greater temptation and facilitation toward sinful behavior. Our mundane concern over "identity theft" pales when compared to Satan's desire to truly steal our human identity.

Lumen Gentium is designed to combat Satan's hijacking of technology. In Lumen Gentium, technology is viewed as gifts given to us by God to foster understanding and unity among all peoples. Digital media, computer animation, interactive displays, virtual, augmented, and mixed reality, lasers, animatronic robotics, and technologies yet to be invented are all brought together as physical expressions of a living faith.

There is also a practical heavenly reason for the construction of Lumen Gentium: it is to be a veritable portal for angels transiting between Heaven and Earth. It is to be a physical connection between Earth and Heaven, in the same way that churches maintain the connection between Jesus and Earth. As we have seen, angels serve myriad purposes in the life of humanity. Jesus oftentimes referenced the legions of angels that would, could, and did attend to his call and command. In the same way that angels are messengers of the Heavenly Father so too is human genius as manifest in technology. Lumen Gentium is the home and gateway of both angelic emissaries and human aspirants.

Lumen Gentium will rise like a crown upon Pittsburgh's riverbank. Designed by renowned architect Louis Astorino, Lumen Gentium's pyramid-like shape is the geometric manifestation of the Holy Trinity, the oneness of Father, Son, and Holy Spirit. The triangular construct of Lumen Gentium also embodies the Trinitarian design of the Chapel of the Holy Spirit in Vatican City, also designed by Louis Astorino.

In appearance, Lumen Gentium is readily identified as a pyramid. This is not coincidence. As we have seen, pyramids serve specific purposes as foci of energy. Lumen Gentium will serve as a giant vortex of love empowering the human spirit to overcome worldly and mortal obstacles and limitations. Its gilded veneer will stand as a golden beacon renewing, energizing the Earth while beckoning visitors. This eminence will also blind fallen angels and render them powerless to negate the blessings emanating from this modern sanctuary and carried away with them by the visiting multitudes.

Those who enter will feel blessed, absorbing the energy emanating from angels perceived yet unseen, energy embodied in the myriad angelic representations adorning its interior. Many will experience peace and joy; others will be healed. There will be no doubt about its spiritual power, nor the heavenly mandate for humanity to become like its Creator.

Lumen Gentium's centerpiece is a great dome, representing eternal life and the heart of God. A giant angel, representative of Pittsburgh's historical prowess, graces the building's pinnacle, towering above an observation deck. Beneath it will be located a conference center where world leaders will be encouraged to come, contemplate, envision, and act upon world peace.

Visitors entering the dome are greeted by two colossal animatronic angels. Between the angels there rests a great globe. Telepresence allows the globe to illuminate the native lands of whosoever approaches, underscoring the oneness of the human family on our planet. On it are also projected real time images of how our world looks in space.

Above the globe, a clock signifies that we are beings in time who already share in eternity, a point punctuated by the choreographed movements of this giant angelic glockenspiel. In keeping with the Divine Plan, we can envision these angels as counting out the time remaining until the end of creation.

This majestic rotunda is encircled with rooms conveying the aspects of the divine mysteries within which all of us live. Visitors may sit and reflect in the Meditation Room, a room of deeply symbolic images and sounds, of myriad tactile and olfactory sensations.

Imagine a living tableau of the human predicament. This is the room for those who are still seeking, for those who are mustering the courage to knock, those looking for existential answers.

In the Marian Room, Earth and Heaven converge. Mary, the Mother of Jesus, is presented as the mother of us all, as intercessor, not only for us as individuals, but for all humanity. Mary is presented as "every woman" whose visage transforms to reflect the many faces of human womanhood. An awe-inspiring visitation by Mary and a choir of angels is created visually over a real time image of Pittsburgh and other earthly regions. Guests are encouraged to pray the rosary to the accompaniment of a choir of gloriously arrayed animatronic angels.

The role and presence of angels in our lives is made most manifest in the Angel Room. Here, myriad animatronic, robotic angels illuminate for us the fact that we are never alone, that we are accompanied at all times by heavenly guardians. They are sent by their Creator, who is also our Creator, to accompany us on our earthly journey, regardless of our duration in this life. This room underscores visually the fact that all human life is sacred and that no child, born or unborn, has ever been abandoned by the Heavenly Father. God accompanies us on every moment of our journey through this life filled with both sorrow and joy.

Music too comes from God and is often said to be the "language of the soul." In Lumen Gentium, music serves as a representation and celebration of the Almighty's desire for harmony. We acknowledge the "music of the spheres"—the tonal vibrations of the planets and stars, sounds likened to those of the "heavenly choir" of cherubim. Lumen Gentium, therefore, offers to young and old alike the opportunity to experience a place where heaven and earth touch as they do in a church.

The Chapel meanwhile is where the "heavy laden" will be given rest, the seekers will be helped to find what they were looking for, and answers will be provided to the questioning. The Chapel Room is unlike any earthly chapel known; for it reflects the joy, peace, and wonderment of the Garden of Eden. It is the "Secret Garden" made manifest, where the gates open verily onto Paradise.

Lumen Gentium combines the reflective majesty of the world's great cathedrals, with the symbolism, wonderment, and vitality found in the finest museums devoted to science, technology, and nature. Its theme is hope and love, but it is not a religious theme park. It celebrates humankind's ability to create technological marvels, but in recognition of the Almighty's omniscience and omnipotence.

It is fitting therefore that Pittsburgh should be the site for this earthly wonder, for Pittsburgh has become synonymous with transformation. The city and its people have weathered many storms and have overcome many hardships and challenges. People from all over the world will travel to Pittsburgh to experience this unique blending of timeless spiritual symbolism and the most modern of technologies. Pittsburgh and Lumen Gentium will give hope to the world.

So what is Lumen Gentium? It is a cathedral for the twenty-first century, the cathedral Leonardo da Vinci would build were he alive today. It is to be a center for peace, hope, and love, featuring visions of worship built around humankind's ability and desire to emulate its Creator. It is right therefore to give thanks and praise for this in a uniquely Pittsburgh way: with iron, steel, glass, robotics, virtual and augmented reality, and the latest of technologies for the highest of Almighty praises. Lumen Gentium's goal is to explore the mysteries of God not to understand them but to enjoy them and to deepen our love for the Almighty.

One of the primary objectives of the revelation and the insights provided to Connie Valenti, given by supernatural inspiration, is specifically the charge of building Lumen Gentium. It is divine motivation that someone reading this opus will experience the calling to help realize this vision. We believe many on Earth will help in the creation of Lumen Gentium, though it is accepted this might be a slow process. Regardless, the Lord will guide and bless progress toward Lumen Gentium. Angels are being formed to help with Lumen Gentium. If you are one of the souls so moved by this invocation, please reach out to us at the URL posted at the start of this book.

Our hope is that this revelation will bring
us closer to our Heavenly Father.

Attribution: Thomas Cole, The Garden of Eden, painting, 1828

THE TENTH CHAPTER

Concluding Thoughts and Admonitions

Truth is a foundational essence of The One. What you have read in this book comes from two celestial tomes. The first belongs to the Great Father. This book contains all wisdom and knowledge. It explains how angel and human seeds of life were created. The other book belongs to the Heavenly Father. This is a book of rules, reflected in the living commandments inspired by the Great Father. It also contains a record of what the Heavenly Father has done.

It is hoped the truths revealed in this revelation will open hearts, minds, and souls, and that these truths will bring people closer to the Heavenly Father. Wonderful things will happen when we take that amazing step. Earth will also open to reveal many of its secrets.

All life is a form of energy. All creation has a soul, a form of living, of sentience: water, rocks, minerals, and even man-made objects like metals. There was a time when we could feel that energy. It will reawaken in us eventually. There are times when we can still sense it, and it makes us feel good and transcendent. Life is not hopeless because of how much we are loved.

It is in this same spirit that Mother Nature, despite her great anger, has not yet given up on humanity. Out of love she is still trying to help humans and animals recognize their shared spirit. She wants them to know they were created to love one another and to live peacefully in close relationship. Preordained as it was in Isaiah: The wolves shall live with lambs. The leopards shall rest with young goats. The calves and young lions shall walk together with a small child to guide them.

Although life is a great mystery, it remains fascinating how The One, in conjunction with Him and the Supreme Creator, works through our weaknesses, failures, and faults to accomplish good in ways we could never imagine. Powerful energies still flow to us from the cross of Jesus. His blood, sweat, tears, and water still mark the Earth.

Angels are still created from the energy Marguerita has given to the Great Father, but no additional human souls will ever be created. Every human soul has already spent at least one lifetime on Earth.

Lessons culminating from this revelation are simple and direct: when evil seems to rule the world, turn away from it. Accept the love of Jesus and Mary. When we pray, Mary and the angels take our petitions first to the Heavenly Father and then to the Great Father. Even though we cannot see it, beautiful energy is released from our heart and soul when we pray. This is the energy she gathers as she transmutes between Heaven and Earth.

When she appears before the Heavenly Father, she bows down with great respect and reverence. She offers him this energy and all the energy expended in prayer from the beginning of time in the form of an enormous brilliant white ball of energy. This energy feeds the Heavenly Father and sustains him in presence and purpose. Never forget the Heavenly Father in your prayers.

Undoubtedly, this revelation has at times proved shocking, difficult for many raised in traditional faith to fathom. Such, though, is the nature of revelation. And yet it also confirms much of what we have always believed. Our universe and all life forms within it were created through the intelligence, power, and, above all, love of The One who oversees all life beyond our Earth.

Does such a discovery and declaration deepen one's faith or weaken it? Might the desire to explore outer space in search for other life forms come from the deepest part of our being? Perhaps this quest stems from a deep-seated intuition that there is indeed more to life than has been revealed to date. Would discovering that life proliferates throughout the universe make it an even more precious and cherished gift? Does all of this lead to fundamental truths that have so far escaped humankind? Only enough truth is given to us as we are able to comprehend at any given time in our human and spiritual evolution. Perhaps the human race is now ready for new truths, but we only have so much time to understand them.

The significant fact is that Lucifer hates the explanations appearing in this inspired account. He does not want us to know about the existence of other heavenly or supernatural beings in the universe and how they interceded in establishing his earthly kingdom. He worries that he and his fallen angels might not be able to travel with us, if and when we seek out and inhabit other planets. In the meantime, he continues to influence people with position, money, power, and sex. He allows them to "play God."

His fears are quite justified: he will never attain his desire to rule both Heaven and Earth. Whether he rules you, however, is up to your free will.

Pope Francis has said, "When our eyes are illumined by the Spirit, they open to contemplate God, in the beauty of nature and in the grandeur of the cosmos, and they lead us to discover how everything speaks to us about Him and His love." Connie Ann Valenti possesses this profound love for God. Throughout her life she has been given this gift of spiritual knowledge illumined by the Holy Spirit. It is a gift that perfects faith and reveals how all of life is related to God.

Her previous book is titled *Stories of Jesus - A Gospel of Faith and Imagination.*

Monsignor Ronald Lengwin has been a talk show host on KDKA radio in Pittsburgh for over forty years. He is fascinated by life's many mysteries, especially the Mystery that God is.

Dr. Donald Marinelli is an educator, theatre practitioner, technology futurist, and Christian existentialist with a lifelong interest in ascertaining God's purpose for humankind.

CPSIA information can be obtained
at www.ICGtesting.com
Printed in the USA
BVHW090625091019
560599BV00004B/14/P